I0690956

The Undying

Mudrooroo

ETT IMPRINT

Exile Bay

This edition published by ETT Imprint, Exile Bay 2021

First published by Angus & Robertson 1998

First electronic edition ETT Imprint 2017.

This book is copyright. Apart from any fair dealing for the purposes of private study, research, criticism or review, as permitted under the Copyright Act, no part may be reproduced by any process without written permission. Inquiries should be addressed to the publishers:

ETT IMPRINT
PO Box R1906
Royal Exchange NSW 1225
Australia

Copyright © Estate of Mudrooroo 2020

ISBN 978-1-922473-46-7 (pbk)

ISBN 978-0-6480963-9-9 (ebk)

Cover: *Native Encampment* by John Skinner Prout
Cover design by Tom Thompson

To my friends and enemies.

This story is fiction and should be treated and read as such.
No reality where none intended.

Mudrooroo was born in Narrogin in Western Australia in 1938. He travelled extensively throughout Australia and the world and lived in Nepal for ten years, then spent the last ten years of his life in Brisbane. He died on January 14 2020. Mudrooroo had been active in Aboriginal cultural affairs, was a Member of the Aboriginal Arts Unit committee of the Australia Council, and a co-founder with Jack Davis of the Aboriginal Writers, Oral Literature and Dramatists Association. He piloted Aboriginal literature courses at Murdoch University, the University of Queensland, the University of the Northern Territory and Bond University. Mudrooroo was a prolific writer of poetry and prose and is best known for his novels, *Wildcat Falling* and *Master of the Ghost Dreaming;* and his critical work, *Writing from the Fringe. Old Fellow Poems* and *Wildcat Falling* are both available with his audio presentation. His last books were the novel *Balga Boy Jackson* in 2017, and the first volume of his memoirs, *Tripping with Jenny* in 2020.

Books by Mudrooroo available in ETT Imprint

Tripping with Jenny
Balga Boy Jackson
Wildcat Falling (ebook)
Doin' Wildcat
Wildcat Screaming (ebook)
Dr Wooreddy's Prescription for Enduring
   the Ending of the World
Long Live Sandawarra
The Indigenous Literature of Australia
The Garden of Gethsemane
An Indecent Obsession (ebook)
Aboriginal Mythology
The Kwinkan (ebook)
The Secret of Hanging Rock
Old Fellow Poems (ebook)

Master of the Ghost Dreaming series:
Bk 1: The Master of the Ghost Dreaming
Bk 2: The Undying
Bk 3: Underground
Bk 4: The Promised Land

CHAPTER ONE

Jangamuttuk, Ludjee, Augustus yale George,
Yenger jarm garana,
Yenger jarm garana.

That's how we begin this songline. We created it on that boat. Those times, long ago, when from the east, from the southeast where our island lives, we came sailing, sailing into the setting sun. We of the rising sun were driven forth, to sail into the setting sun. That's what lies behind this, this song verse. Jangamuttuk, Ludjee and me, her son George, with the few remaining blackfellows of our mob, we came close to this land. On our right side, it receded ever westwards, ever westwards towards the setting sun blazing a coiled serpent across our bows as we sailed on and on, until I reached here alone and unwanted.

I, the stranger with strange habits which make me avoid the full light of day, enter into the warm circle of your fire and will exchange my yarn for your company. It is all that I have, all that I, the undying, have left at the end of that western voyage. Hard and long was the sailing, truly terrifying were our adventures as one by one we succumbed to the toil. Often we thought it would never end, and for many it did not. Now across the milky ocean in the sky, they sail on, leaving me alone with my tales, with the discomfort of the end of Jangamuttuk's vision. He, my father, our shaman, the dreamer of visions which receded as we sailed westwards, ever westwards until we became as ghosts and ghosts became real men and women. My father, Master of the Ghost Dreaming, sang his ghost songs which were to release us from the domain of the ghosts, which were to close the gate leading from the ghostland to our world, but he failed and wherever we hesitated, wherever we stopped to rest, there were they. Worse, far worse, at least for me, an old granny ghost touched me with her teeth and followed after us. She gave me dreams that were not my dreams, and that is part of my story.

We were a small band of blackfellows, twenty in all, fleeing on a schooner from our island exile. Our homeland had been invaded and we were dispossessed of our hunting grounds. We despaired for our very lives, then the ghost Fada came to us and said that he would save us. He took us to a small island where we languished and died. Fada ate at our souls and, when he had finished eating, he abandoned us. It would have been the end of all of us, but then Jangamuttuk recovered his powers and discovered the Ghost Dreaming. Our shaman, my father, strong in his ceremonies, keen in the visions of his songs, sang Wadawaka to us – he who was born on the water and knew the ways of the sea. Wadawaka accepted us and captained our schooner which sailed on and on with the long stretch of land ever hazy on our right. His vision was beyond the stretch of land, far beyond, and he told me that his beginning had been Africa, though what his end would be he refused to say, though he too was a seer of visions.

> *Wadawaka inenanam modjie modie.*
> *Djurin nana gulara bidin.*
> *Dabor inganj bidin*
> *Djao djao.*

He came up from the sea, from the cool, cool sea he rose to hurry us west. He kept us going in that long boat, in that ship hung with shrouds which rattled in the breeze like dead men's bones, and when the wind howled through the rigging there came from them the shook-shook of giant bat wings. How that sound echoes in my mind, but from another and later time. Then it was but the sound of the sails. Now it seems to be all around me as huge dark wings, lifting and flying me back to when I was not a stranger, but with my own mob.

Now they are gone, and I sit at your campfire and sing and yarn to you. I watch you nod your heads as you listen to my story, to my songs which are akin to your own, though they are in my own language kept alive in my head. Our people, my mob, are gone and there is no one left to talk to in those ancient words. My language falls into the swirls of the prow breaking through that sea, ever westwards until the land ends, as my people, my language, ends. Now I must use the language of the ghosts and let it shape my lips. I must breathe forth their words as I let the power of the Ghost Dreaming move me along. Ah, that long voyage, each part a verse of a song singing us along. The songline ends here with me, the last of my mob. No, I do not want tea. I want your ears so that I can tell you of those days which we thought belonged to us, for we were powerful in song.

And you wish to know my name? Yes, my name. It was given to me by my father, Jangamuttuk, as I sat in the cave with him and he sang out my destiny. Jangamuttuk, father, shaman of our mob. Well, my name is George. I was named after a mad king and my elder brother, Augustus, was named after an insane emperor and also after the ghost Fada who ruled over us on that island, ever imprisoning us in the words he drew on paper. He scribbled and sketched while we died and died, then Jangamuttuk awoke to his visions and entered them to find a path for us to follow. Whether it was the wrong or right way, it does not matter now, for at the time it gave us the strength to sail into the setting sun, coiling and uncoiling a giant serpent that drew us towards its golden land, though Fada took a last victim as we cleared the island.

My poor brother Augustus was faint .of heart and body and had listened to Fada overmuch. With the island still in his sight, he fell from the masthead up which he had clambered for one last lingering look. How we mourned, and I can still feel those tears on my cheeks. It was then that the sails began to sound like the rattle of dead men's bones, my brother's bones. It was then that Wadawaka saw my distress and became an elder brother to me. He told and showed me things that stood me in good stead in the long days ahead.

You ask how I survived? It was fate first, in the kindness of Wadawaka, then in the shape of a female, that old yet young granny, who followed after us and passed over to me her ghost ways. I cannot bear the sun. Now I seek the quiet coolness of the night and remember her in the shook-shook sound of giant bat wings. Shrouds of our sails, giant bat wings drawing us ever westwards. My father's vision and her vision have joined, leaving me alone and forsaken. My mob are all gone and I live on. I, the undying, live on, though what life could I have when the voyage finally ended with the death of all those I held dear? Worse, all that remained of those days was her, and she was waiting for me in this land under the sun, though she lived under the moon. Yes, she waited for me with the gift of the eternal wanderer. She followed us during the time of this tale, trudging across the land by night, resting in dark places by day. She followed us while we fled in that schooner with a pensive Wadawaka at the helm and with sails shuddering like the shrouds of corpses and calling out shook-shook to her ... But I get beyond myself. This is not about that at all. It is about my father, Jangamuttuk, and my womb mother, Ludjee. It is about Wadawaka who knew the secrets of walking on water and made us all walk on water as my father sang us along ever westwards, away from our island home. It is also about her, but enough of her. I begin my tale.

Bright with hope was the day. Wadawaka told us to heave the anchor and bright was the western sun coiled glowing in the sky as we sailed from the island. We felt the wind fill our sails and thrust us towards our hope. They did not sound like bats' wings then, but like the sweet moan of the didgeridoo. Jangamuttuk took up his clapsticks and sang us towards what we hoped would be our new home.

Jun inangan bururu jen;
Dumbar innjan;
Innjan gurwal gun burgalgal.

'It flies away, flying, away, straight it goes.' The verse sang us straight towards the sun glowing before us, a great serpent, always writhing, always restless, always filled with the promise of the new home. Such was our hope in those faraway days, those days of flight and adventure. I was young then, without a beard and just past the manhood tests. Yes, just past the manhood business, as was my brother who dived into the sea and found a new home beneath the waves. I covered my anguish at his loss by learning how to propel the vessel through the waves. I pulled on ropes and hoisted and furled sails. Wadawaka taught me how to hold the wheel steady in my hands, to run before the wind and tack across it. Yes, and I was glad that the work was hectic and needed my full concentration. There was no time for moping for the strait through which we fled was an unruly passageway, as unruly as the open ocean beyond. The waters boiled and battered and sought to have their own way with us. My arms grew strong in keeping the vessel pointed westwards, but they were not strong enough when an ice-cold gale hurled in from the southeast to seize the rudder. Helpless before it, we were driven north towards that long hazy length of coast.

My grip weakened as under bare sticks we charged towards that coastline, now hidden in swirling fog and mist. My blood grew cold, then surged in my veins as the fog roiled before the gale, twisting into the shapes of gigantic sea monsters. My terror was not hard to understand, for all that I had ever known until then was an island I could cross in a day. Now, in front of my eyes, was not only the storm-tossed sea but a land suddenly revealed to stretch east and west, seemingly without end. Our little schooner hurtled towards it, towards a jutting point of its mass, and even Jangamuttuk's chant was swept away in contempt by the blast of the storm. Powerless, he retreated down below, while I remained to strain at the wheel. It spun in my burning fists as the tempest switched its attack from due south. Wadawaka rushed to take the helm. We both clung to it, as our vessel rushed upon the coast. Was our voyage at an end? The waters swirled in a white froth directly in front of our bows. Our schooner shuddered from stem to stern as the gale blasted us from starboard. Our jib flapped for a long moment, then ripped to shreds streaming to port uselessly. The wind howled in triumph, then suddenly moaned in dismay as we came under the lea of the rocky point and it lost its prey. Yet the danger was not over, for now a current seized us to hurl us on towards the land. Wadawaka shouted in vain for the remains of the jib to be cut away, but his crew were sheltering below, perhaps cowering in fear.

'Not even a song now to bring us to safety,' he shouted at me, exulting in the danger. He stared at the water, judging the current. 'Gently to starboard,' he called. I gave the wheel a half turn and the vessel was guided towards where the point met the long curve of a bay. 'Right, now steady as she goes.' Wadawaka ran to the bow, unsecured the anchor, then released the chock on the capstan. The anchor rattled down to the bottom and held. We swung to a rest close to a land which seemed to be brooding over accepting our presence.

My father returned to the deck, glanced ashore, gave a loud cooee and sang a verse of welcome. It was then that the heavy swell subsided as the wind turned to blow as a breeze from the land. It brought with it the scents of animals and plants, some of which were familiar to me.

Jangamuttuk inenanan modje Indedenan
wadejan
Injele laib wamberanj
Laibe yan wamberanj imbegandanan;
Reb wambe gadjan yonennolenan.

'Jangamuttuk comes to the north. He sees good people there. These he keeps. The bad ones he throws away.' So sang Jangamuttuk, carefully securing us from harm with his magic as we went ashore. The land sighed as it accepted his song, as it perhaps accepted us. My fears fell away, for we were strong in our faith in his vision and songs. I watched as my father and mother seated themselves on the sand at the base of the steep cliff which barred our way inland. I stared as they entered a trance and left us. Their bodies remained as still as corpses, as if waiting to receive the purifying flame. Wadawaka glanced at them and shook his locks, which in our tribal fashion were daubed with red ochre, then, always practical, began setting up a camp. He was constantly active, always doing things. His heavy physique moved with an economy of skill which came from experience. The rest of us pitched in, using everyday actions to push away any disquiet in our minds. There was enough driftwood at the base of the cliff to provide fuel. Flint struck against steel and soon we had a fire going. Wadawaka deftly rolled johnny cakes from flour and placed them on a flat piece of iron to cook. I looked up as a shiver passed over Father's and Mother's bodies. Their eyes brightened and Jangamuttuk exclaimed at the sight of the damper, 'Had enough of those burnt dust things. I've been out over the land and soon we'll have some better tucker. I've seen wallabies on a hillside, kangaroos on the plains, possums in the trees and not too far away either – that way.' And he pursed the left side of his mouth to show the direction.

'But as I flew, I hesitated at a tree and from it came the sound of laughter. A long and fierce cackling. It is best that we remain on our guard, for this land is strange to us, it is not our land,' Ludjee cautioned.

'And I saw giant birds roaming about in huge flocks,' Jangamuttuk said, then added, 'But beyond there was a slight smell of ghosts, though no sign of them. There were old camps of blackfellows, but I saw never a one.'

'But they must be here,' I broke in, pointing at a midden. 'Look at that pile of shells. They were not heaped up like that by sea birds.'

'Oh, we will meet them in time and they will welcome us as a long lost mob,' Jangamuttuk informed us. 'This land is not so unknown to us. Is there not the story about how we came from a vast land to the north, then there came a mighty flood and our country became separated and we marooned? We are not like this Wadawaka, we were made in the land and not on the sea.' He smiled and glanced slyly at the man squatting beside the fire, who lifted his eyes from his cooking.

'I was born on the waters, but Africa is the land of my mother's birth,' Wadawaka retorted. 'It is far far away and the animals are not as these, though I too have heard of a giant bird which cannot fly. My mother told me that Hyena, the dog-faced one, tricked him into eating stones and he became so heavy that he could not fly.'

I listened to them and decided that one day I would ask Wadawaka about this Africa of his mother's birth, for all I knew was an island and now this short length of beach. What other wonders, I thought, rested beyond the horizon? Why, I thought, there might even be fish that flew through the air or walked on land. Yes, then I was still young and green. I did not even know that when my mother and father entered a trance they rode their dreaming animals to fly through the air. Dreaming animals, you ask? These too are part of my story and they will enter my yarn at the proper place. All that you need know now is that my parents had psychically scouted out the land, looking for any dangers which might threaten us. They had even found a track leading off the beach.

The solid feel of the earth beneath our feet had revived our spirits. After our days on the schooner, our stomachs rumbled for fresh meat and it was quickly decided that we would go on a hunt for some of those animals my father had seen. Wadawaka rowed out to the schooner and came back with the few ghost weapons we had. Jangamuttuk had gone with him and came back with an armful of spears. While Wadawaka checked the priming of the guns and loaded them, Jangamuttuk ran his hands over the wooden shafts which had come from our previous home. The sea air had warped some of them and these he discarded. The others he handed out, one to each of the twelve men, telling them what needed to be repaired. Most of the wooden points were blunt and needed to be sharpened. In some cases the barb also had become loose and had to be tightened. He grumbled to us that in the old days the barb had been placed in a notch made for it, then bound with wet kangaroo sinew which dried to hold it securely in place. This was not possible to do now and so a thin leather thong was used instead. Wadawaka shouldered a musket and handed me a pistol. I got to my feet and waited for my father to lead the way off the beach.

'Arrh, this earth is strong,' he exclaimed, stamping his feet. 'It does not move as that boat did and, best of all, I have one of these in my hands again.'

He chuckled as he weighed the spear in his hand, testing the balance, then poised it before making his cast. Although old, his arm was still strong and the shaft sped along the beach for about fifty metres then skidded along for another twenty. He gestured at a spear which lay at his feet and ordered me to throw it. On the island, we had had little use for spears. In fact, Fada had forbidden their possession and one night had collected those which were not hidden and burnt them. I had only thrown a spear about twice before so my stance was ungainly and my throw worse. A flush of blood came over my face, but who needed one of these unwieldy lengths of wood when I had a pistol? During the calm days on the ocean Wadawaka had taught me how to aim and fire it until I could hit a small fragment of wood tossed from the bow and bobbing past the schooner's side.

But my father clung to the old ways and weapons and did not understand such things as pistols and muskets. He growled, 'Good time and place for this young one to learn how to use a spear, instead of that noisy ghost pistol which will scare away any animal within a cooee of us.' He indicated with. a toss of his beard the spear I had thrown, then said with a chuckle, 'His skill is such that he'd have to get right up to an old man kangaroo whose ears have been blocked up with age and even then he'd have to use his spear as· a waddy and club him.' But then his words left him and his face clouded over with sadness. I realised that he was thinking of his other son whom he could never teach. He looked from woman to woman and I felt his sadness. I was the only young one there and none of the women were in the family way. He tugged at his grey beard to fend off his tears. I was the only one he could teach and pass his knowledge to. He turned his eyes back to me and to cheer him up I declared, 'I can use this!' I waved my pistol, cocked it and, aiming at a shell, pulled the trigger. There was a flash in the pan. To my dismay the pistol had misfired.

'So much for that thing,' Jangamuttuk growled, recovering his spirits at the mishap. He watched as I reprimed the weapon and said, 'And beware of using it in the hunt, for the noise is like thunder. Remember, we are in a strange land where huge birds run instead of fly and spirits laugh at us from trees. Tread lightly and leave few tracks. Speak more with your body than your mouth. Time enough for noise when we are made welcome. Now, learn to use this.' He thrust his spear into my hands.

'And while you men play with your spears and hopefully get us some rich red meat, we women will scour the sand for pippies and clams. That rocky point should have mussels too. So off to your hunt and we'll go to our gathering.' Mother broke in to move Father's thoughts further away from his grief. She was not a dreamer or singer of songs and was able to put things quickly behind her and get on with life. And this seemed to be the case now, for even though only a short time ago Augustus had died and the mourning period was still in effect – her hair was just beginning to grow back after she had shaved her head as was the custom – she had resumed her cheery no-nonsense self. Though perhaps she was only hiding her feelings, for she exchanged a long look of commiseration with her husband before leading the group of women off along the beach. As if to show that he had recovered his spirits, he called after her, 'Perhaps you should take him along with you. He is more like a daughter than a son.'

My mother did not reply or even look back. Determinedly, she led the group of women along the beach. They kept their eyes on the ground and every now and again stopped to dig with their toes, unveiling a pippy which they threw into the sack they carried with them. While the women moved towards where the rocky point entered the sea, Jangamuttuk now led us towards its base. He stopped to check the contents of the sack and tried one of the pippies. He pronounced it 'delicious', then continued on to where we could scramble onto a steeply angled rock face that rose up to the top of the point. He moved slowly as his joints had stiffened with age, and we kept behind him out of respect. Also, he was our strength and able to face whatever might be at the cliff top.

The backbone of the point gradually bent up to the level of the land and then merged with it. We came up onto a wide plain, grey and hard, that stretched away from our eyes to the far horizon. It lacked the serrated appearance of our own island and seemed, at least to me, an infinitude of flatness with nothing much to describe about it. I was relieved at last to find some distinctions to rest my gaze on, a few smooth hillocks which broke the monotony on the northwest horizon. Jangamuttuk wended his way through tussocks of low grass which grew scattered over the featureless grey and tugged and scratched our legs as we followed in his footsteps. He moved even more slowly now, not because he was treading carefully to avoid the sharp grass blades, but because he insisted on explaining the techniques of spear throwing to me, stopping every now and again to demonstrate the proper stance and cast so that we moved together rather than in single file.

After the tenth time he had done this, he tossed me the heavy spear and, as I went along, I practised my stance and cast. The wooden point had become blunt and the barb loose by the time we reached the base of one of the hillocks. From a distance, it had appeared smooth and round, but now I saw that it was a heap of boulders on the featureless plain.

'Good for rock wallaby,' Jangamuttuk grunted, then gestured for me to fix my spear. I scraped the point on a surface of a boulder until it was somewhat sharper, then sought to tighten the barb by twisting a stick in the cord until it felt secure. Jangamuttuk took a look and laughed. 'Haven't you heard about Crow and Eagle? In the old days they went hunting and Eagle, he the sly one, had his barb slanting back shaftwards and Crow, the silly one, had his slanting pointwards. Well, when Eagle flung his spear, it entered an animal and stuck there, but when Crow cast his, it came out easily and the animal got away. So be clever Eagle and not stupid Crow, if you can.'

I fixed the barb until it pointed towards my hand while Jangamuttuk stared at the pile of boulders and softly sang a verse to bring us luck. 'Now,' he said to me, 'in the hunt you don't talk, you use the language of signs. Those wallaby don't have big ears for nothing and they're always inquisitive about the language of men. Once, it is said, they were the only ones that had language and we stole it from them. They still remember it, though they can no longer speak, and they listen in an attempt to get it back, so we must use gestures to confuse them. They see us making these signs and try to make out their meaning. They forget themselves as they watch us, then whammo, those wallabies learn something else.'

He showed me the signs. 'Wallaby' was denoted by both hands held open to the sides of the head, denoting the big ears of the animal. Slight movements of the hands showed that the animal was suspicious, still hands that he was not. The flat of the hand held over the mouth indicated silence. 'Stay, be still' was a gesture at the person and the fall of the arm. 'Spearing' was simply the clutching of an imaginary spear and a slight forward motion of the hand.

He gave me other signs such as go that way or this way and so on, then said, 'These are but the rudiments of sign language. They will be enough for this hunt, but with all that time to fill in on that boat I'll teach you the whole grammar by and by. Body language is as complicated as mouth language. What you speak, I can gesture,' he said, acting out a mime to illustrate. Then, grinning at my smile, he added, 'If you could hear that, you would not be amused. Now, let us go and kill our meat, though I think that I would like these better than those.' And he spoke again in a flutter of gestures, then laughed at my perplexed face.

Jangamuttuk turned and made his way up the hill. As he climbed he began to speak with his body. His signs directed our advance into and up the hillock. I crept through the rocks and boulders, feeling the coolness of the stone under the soles of my feet for the day was cloudy and the rocks still damp from the rains of the squall which had driven us into the shelter of the headland. A gesture told me to stop. Hands to the head indicated a rock wallaby. Motionless ears informed me that he was unaware of our presence. An arm told me to raise my spear and get ready for the cast. I did so very slowly and carefully, anxious to please my father as well as to not make a sound as my eyes searched for the animal. There he was, between those two boulders falling to the left and right to form a cleft in which a few tufts of grass grew. His ears pointed towards me. I flung my spear just as the wallaby bounded to the left – and into the flashing shaft of Jangamuttuk.

'Watch them ears, boy. They'll tell you which way he's going to jump, and that'll be into your spear as long as you're aware and quick.'

His advice flowed over me throughout the day and by the time the sun, a glowing patch through the clouds, was halfway down the sky I had speared my first wallaby. Overall our tally was six. We piled them on the flat surface of a boulder, then Jangamuttuk gestured for us to continue up to the summit. There we gazed over the plain which went on and on until it fell over the horizon. It was so vast and flat that it caused in me (and the others) a vertigo of the spirit which made me long for my small and contained island home. I felt as tiny and as powerless as an ant. This land was much too much for me. To quell my dizziness, I turned my eyes to the familiar sea which, under Wadawaka's tutelage, I was beginning to know. There, anchored beside the headland, was my friend the schooner. My fingers clenched around an imaginary wheel as I felt her surge and move beneath me. Home and security. There was Wadawaka hard at work at the bow, and from the beach rose the smoke of our fire blending into the cloudy sky so that it did not call attention to itself. The women were clustered about the fire and there ...

'Look!' Jangamuttuk exclaimed, bringing me back to him and the land. He raised an arm, indicating a thin column of smoke rising on the horizon. It could just be discerned against the cloudy sky. 'People there, two, no, three walks away at the most. They'll see our smoke too if their eyes are as good as mine. Perhaps they'll come for a visit, see who we are. Perhaps I'll go and visit them on Goanna. Blackfellow's fire at least,' he growled at me. 'Mark out how the smoke rises, thin and straight as one of our women's legs. If they were *nam*, ghosts, their smoke would billow up like a cloud or fog hugging the ground. They do it like that because their skins can't take the full light of the sun, but no ghosts walk or sit close by. Could smell them on the wind if there were.' And he sniffed in all four directions, testing the air.

But, and I could not escape the thought, what would we have done if he *had* smelt the *nam*, those ghosts who had dispossessed us of our land, hunting and killing us until they had reduced our numbers so that we could all fit onto one small schooner? Twenty souls in all, twelve men and eight women and, after the death of my brother, I was the only young one left. Tears came into my eyes as I thought over how pitifully few we were. A few survivors fleeing westwards on a stolen schooner, riding the waves and the songs of Jangamuttuk's vision which was supposed to bring us to our promised land under the coils of the setting sun. But what would we really find there, if we ever arrived?

Doubts as these began when we arose one morning to find that our didgeridoo player, Wawilak, was missing from our vessel. He had vanished in the night. The women wailed and pounded their heads on the deck at this catastrophe. Wadawaka tacked the schooner back over his course. He even took his *abeng*, his ram's horn trumpet, and blew loud blasts over the sea. Jangamuttuk and Ludjee entered their trance state but even then could not find him. They returned to say that he was not to be seen, that behind us a fog clung to the sea and a huge crag of frozen water floated like a ghost fortress there. Worse, far worse, they reported that ahead, in the west, they had seen six large ghost ships coming towards us. My father's ceremonies had been performed to close the gates between our land and the ghostland, but if there were six large ghost ships ahead, coming towards us, this must mean that they were still open. Sadly, we performed the burial ceremony for Wawilak, covering our bodies with ashes and seeking to send his soul to rest. Jangamuttuk sang his death song, then broke into the ghost song as those musicians who had learnt their instrument from him cast them into the sea. The wooden tubes floated away from us, a visible loss of culture as we sailed away towards the west where the old would be reformed in a new land.

These thoughts of mine circled about a core of emotion which hardened and changed during the voyage and the journey became more real to me than its phantasised end. Perhaps my father too came to realise this, that the end did not matter as much as the verses of the songline which extended out and beyond this plane of being. In other and older songlines the ancestor came down to this earth, travelled across it, had his adventures, then departed back into the sky from whence he had come, leaving only the songs of his adventures behind. Perhaps my father operated like these ancestors on a different plane of seeing, for never did we escape the influence of the ghosts. His ceremonies, though they gave us hope, seemed on reflection to have had the opposite effect to that intended. Instead of closing the entrance to the ghostworld, they seemed to have widened it. Ghosts, released from their world, flooded forth on great wooden ships to drift along the coastlines. They landed and made their homes, as they had on our island. Our island, which had felt the brunt of their invasion. And perhaps, now that they had made it their own, they were following us to make this whole vast land theirs. Eventually this is what happened, but back then did I think such thoughts, or did I merely feel them, as I felt the soft fur of the two wallabies I was carrying through the holes in my ragged ghost shirt? Yes, I think that is how it was. The feelings really began with the death of my brother Augustus, and grew with the disappearance of Wawilak. They flowed forth from the two furry corpses I was carrying on my shoulders, one of which I had slain. I felt their heat departing and the coldness which comes at the loss of the spirit stiffened their bodies. The warm blood from where the spear had ripped through fur into the soft flesh beneath cooled, pooled and congealed. Soon it would freeze solid, but as yet it dripped forth, spreading over my shoulder like the red of the sun spreads over the clouds at sunset. My hand was soon covered with the rich redness of life. I shifted my load and grip so that I could sip at the warm blood as I walked along, tasting in it my future, the salt of the sea and the sweet ashes of the land. It caused me to flow with a desire that I could not give a name to, which replaced the apprehension I had been feeling since we had reached the summit of that rock pile.

I was hot and flushed from a fever by the time I came to the camp where the women were sitting and snacking on the shellfish. Ludjee, my mother, glanced at me and her eyes filled with concern. She came to me and took the two corpses from my back. 'This boy has a fever,' she declared.

Jangamuttuk laughed a harsh laugh as he said, 'And so he should, for today he has been blooded. He has taken his first life, and with a spear, not with that stick which goes crack-crack like my clapsticks and scares everything away. He shall eat of his skill this day and his fever will leave him, for it comes from the blood he has taken -and sampled,' he added, noticing the red on my lips.

'Well, let him eat of the fruits of my gathering first,' she said. 'The sea gives up its food easily here and the mussels are succulent. They will make the boy as strong as any land meat and keep away any evil here.'

I managed to gulp one down, but the taste for sea things had left me. I could hardly wait to rip into the flesh of my prey. Indeed I had become a man with my first kill, and I knew it would not be my last.

I was not alone in my desire for fresh meat. All of us were hungry for it after the salt tack we had been eating on the schooner. I felt saliva rise into my mouth as I watched Jangamuttuk and the other men scoop out a hollow in the sand and line it with stones. They were about to lay two of the wallabies in it when Wadawaka intervened and said, 'You fellows might cook them like that, but it will be better if we skin them first. I could then tan the skins and make jackets out of them. Who knows what the weather will be like further along, and even in the worst of it someone has to be on deck and at the helm.'

Without waiting for a reply, he deftly cut around the throat and legs, slashed down the front and· pulled at the skin. The others watched. I bent and held the carcase for him. The skin slipped off easily, as did the other. He was about to go further and gut the wallabies when Jangamuttuk stopped him. 'We like the insides just as much as the red meat,' he said. 'Stomach contents are our vegetables. We can digest the grass after they have done the first bit. Old man's tucker, you know.'

The carcases were laid in the pit and hot coals placed over them, then more firewood heaped on to keep the heat going. After an hour or so, when the fire had died down, the coals were scraped aside and the carcases pulled out. They were placed on a piece of canvas and Jangamuttuk, because of his seniority, took charge. He propped the carcases on their backs, hacked open the chests and spread them so that the insides were showing. The men scooped up the curdled blood and ate it, then Jangamuttuk drank the gravy of the stomach contents. After this, he hacked up the meat and gave each person a piece or two. I received the end of a tail and then, best of all, the heart. The animal had been young and the muscle was tender enough for my teeth to rip into. It was barely cooked and succulent with blood. I chewed away. The sweet juices dripped from the corners of my mouth. Indeed, as I ate I could feel my fever leaving me.

'We'll get possum tomorrow, easier for old ones like me to digest. This wallaby is a bit tough for worn-down teeth to chew,' Jangamuttuk declared from around the rib bone he was gnawing on.

Wadawaka used a knife to pare meat off a thigh bone and, while chewing it, stared at the other carcasses. He swallowed, then said, 'We can get more of these and salt them for the voyage ahead. We need to use these ghost methods if we are to have meat to eat along our way. Simple job. I've salt enough and a few spare casks. Maybe I could start with one of these while there is still light.' He glanced at the sun where it glowered through the clouds, then suddenly stared hard along the beach. I followed the direction of his gaze. A mob of strange blackfellows were coming towards us. I looked the other way and there was another lot coming along there too. Their spears were raised in their right hands and they held short flat wooden boards in front of them with their left. Between them, we were trapped.

Trapped! Was this to be the end of our voyage? What could we do? The stone points of their spears moved to cover each of us, including the women. I felt for my pistol which I had tucked in the band of my ragged trousers. I raised it and sighted on the leader of the nearest mob, but Jangamuttuk made a gesture for me to put down my weapon. Slowly he got to his feet and walked over to the nearest mob. It was led by a gnarled old fellow with a long grey beard and long hair tied up in a topknot like the tufts of grass which had scratched our legs. The group stopped, but kept their weapons ready. My father stopped a few feet away from them. We looked up at him, not daring to get to our feet. We were vastly outnumbered and now surrounded, for the other mob had drifted around to hem us in. Would they, I wondered, take us for blackfellows? We still were clad in our ghost clothing, somewhat worse for wear, but they were naked and covered in white ash without a trace of red ochre anywhere. So unlike our old traditions of smearing our bodies with a mixture of fat and red ochre. At the mission Fada had forbidden us to do this, and had even tried to get us to keep our hair short, but now that he was gone our locks had grown and we still used the red ointment to colour and shape them.

'Maybe we should not worry overmuch,' Ludjee muttered in a

whisper. 'Since women are here, they will know that we are not a raiding party. Then, there is another sign. In the old days when our men fought, in the excitement their penises rose along with their spears. It was such a sight that no wonder they didn't want the womenfolk along. Now look at theirs – not much of a weapon, are they? Limp as our men's are, but not from fear. Probably from curiosity. Anyway, my husband will smooth the way. He has a way about him. Remember him and Fada? That was a sight to see. He was the only one that could get through to that ghost.'

Her words cheered us up, but our eyes remained glued on Jangamuttuk as he stood there facing the old man who now began chewing his beard as if in anger. At the same time his head bobbed up and down so that he looked like some sort of scrawny bird engaged in a mating dance. My father, our shaman, now made his move, taking off his clothing to reveal the scarring across his chest and also the painted design of his totemic animal which he always wore for protection. The old man glared at him as he stripped. He stared at his markings, then clapped his shield against his spear like an exclamation. Still not a word had been spoken. We were the focus of their eyes. We huddled in a group and stared up at them. At least, as Ludjee had pointed out, their pricks were limp, but not their spears which were in full erection and directed at us.

It was then that Jangamuttuk began to use body language in an effort to communicate with the strangers. He dragged his foot through the sand, making a line which went to the schooner. He cupped his hands many times, then inclined his head into the palm of his hand while rocking his body from side to side. He clutched his beard, spread his fingers across his scarred chest, then pointed at Ludjee and fashioned heavy breasts on his chest. He pointed at me, then at the imaginary breasts. He mimed the action of a musket firing, then got into a spear stance and threw an imaginary spear many times. He dropped to the ground and lay still as if in death. He rose to his feet, went to the fire and picked up some ashes. His hand came up to his face as if miming a snout and then came away. His face was covered with ash and he mimed the firing of a musket again. He sank to his knees as if in terror, got up, ran a few steps, then rocked on his heels while gesturing at the others. His face assumed the lines of an ancient sorrow as his hands mimed movements which seemed to indicate men, women and children. He sank down upon the ground in an attitude of death, then arose and extended a hand flat out, turning it down to show that it was empty. Finally, he gave a shrug, then stood and waited for a response. He even risked glancing back at us, his eyes meeting mine as if to say, 'That's how you use body language, boy'.

Whether this strange mob had understood or not was a moot point. It did cause them to relax their aggressive stance. Many of the men smiled and the old man scowled as if to hide his amusement. His spear came down and the other men, observing this, also lowered their weapons. A few of them even exchanged glances, shrugged and grinned.

'*Munno ngo munguni maro pityuri ngo jungi eno uta,*' the old man growled, which in one of our dialects meant, 'This old man is silly in the head'.

Jangamuttuk replied, '*Tuari ena moolka ena yatea impa,*' which meant, 'You are climbing up a tall gumtree', that is, barking up the wrong tree.

It was a mild insult and the old fellow gestured with his spear, chewed his beard furiously and shouted for us to 'begone'. This resulted in a furious clashing of spears against shields, but it was mere play-acting for even while they were doing this the men were narrowing their circle closer to us, their eyes on the remaining wallabies. Jangamuttuk's reply in their language had broken the tension. In a matter of minutes, they had accepted us as weird blackfellows, a mob who might have come from a far distance, but were related to them at least by language. Soon they were sitting down with us around the fire while the remaining wallabies were prepared for cooking. Waai, for such was the old man's name, took over the cooking, hopping about and bobbing his tuft as he cut open the wallabies and placed the stones within their body cavities. This he told us would hasten the cooking, but Waai meant Crow and we remembered our stories about the stupidity of crows and smiled as he did so. After all, we as members of the Eagle sections belonged to the Eaglehawk ancestor who had invented the shaftward-facing barb, while Crow had the point-facing barb. Eaglehawk had even given Crow his black colour and condemned him to eat carrion, so we did not take umbrage when they laughed long and loudly over my father's body language, though Jangamuttuk did become sullen at this, then angry. He tugged at his locks and got to his feet, his heavy spear in hand. Waai quickly apologised for them, saying that it was only natural to be amused at our strange ways and dialect. This was true, for their language was similar but not quite identical to ours, and as for sign language, they lacked the rudiments of it. Their language in our ears was just as ill-sounding with a mixture of strange words and turns of phrases that sometimes kept us guessing at the meaning, especially as some of their words had meanings the opposite of ours. Still, all in all, we were accepted as guests who spoke a quaint dialect and had equally quaint ways, and as they accepted us we accepted them.

CHAPTER TWO

A ceremony often started with a feeling of sadness for those who were no longer with us, and so it was this night. My brother Augustus was almost a visual presence in my mind, and I knew that we all were remembering Wawilak and his didgeridoo whose soaring notes would quickly have lifted us above the realm of grief and sadness and into that of joyful participation. Now memories of those days of exile on the island came to plague us and our present position added to our melancholy. We were strangers in a strange land which was only a way stop in our voyage. We moped on until the sharp crack-crack of Jangamuttuk's clapsticks sounded out in an effort to push such thoughts away.

The rap-rap, rap-rap of the Master of the Ghost Dreaming's clapsticks called forth the dancers. Eight of our men took up positions next to the women. The men had discarded their ragged ghost clothing and were naked except for the incised pubic shell with designs which once had signified the strong clans of our people. But many clans were not represented now and of the few remaining most had only one or two members. So many of our clans had become extinct or teetered on the edge of extinction, but Jangamuttuk had carefully kept the emblems of these clans and carried them aboard the schooner. Now they were piled beside him, symbolising that they still existed in the Dreaming state. The women, at Fada's constant haranguing – 'You must become civilised; you must keep on your clothing' – had discovered nakedness and shame. Thus they kept on their long Mother Hubbard mission skirts, but were bare above the waist. Their skins had been painted in a lattice work of white lines, which signified a bodice, and even a necklace had been fashioned around their necks with a pearl between their breasts. Three white rows of dots flowed dripping down to the three cicatrices of womanhood which passed across their cleavages. To complete the costume leafy twigs had been plaited into their hair which had been roughly modelled to resemble ghost female hats.

The men had their hair piled up around a piece of wood or tightly rolled-up cloth to signify the shako of a ghost soldier and their bodies were covered with red and white colours in the fashion of the red army jacket. One had the chevrons of a sergeant painted on his arm and others even had buttons and pockets fashioned on their chests.

Jangamuttuk, Master of the Ghost Dreaming and master of ceremonies, was resplendent in the symbols of the ghost civilian clothing

Fada had worn when superintendent of the mission. A crosshatched design of red and white encircled his neck and below this were painted the broad lapels of a frock coat from the vee of which the top of a waistcoat peeped out. His legs, as were the legs of the dancers, were painted white with a circular design at the knee.

Now the Master of the Ghost Dreaming held his clapsticks up to his mouth and whispered to them, then began a rhythm which, in previous versions of the ceremony, had been taken up by Wawilak and the other didgeridoo players giving it volume and substance. Without them, the rhythm was lacking in force. The male and female dancers began a reel as Jangamuttuk began to sing in the ghost language.

> They made of me
> A ghost down under,
> Made for me
> A place to plunder,
> A place to plunder,
> Way down under.

And so the public and truncated version of our ceremony continued. We were performing it as a gift from guests. At our own closed performances, it had eventually wandered into a shamanistic trance in which all participated in the Dreaming. This was not to happen here and it might have been a tame affair if Jangamuttuk had not devised a dramatic ending. He had daubed my body all over with charcoal and whitened my face, hands and feet with pipeclay, then had ordered me to remain hidden at the edge of the clearing in which we were performing. My father now cracked his sticks furiously and began a rushed chant playing on the ghost words:

> Under, plunder, thunder;
> Way may, nay stay;
> Down town under;
> Ghost, ghost under;
> Slam, clam ram blam.

This was my signal to enter the clearing, high stepping to a rat-a-tat marching beat. I marked time before the central fire, then broke my step as the rhythm increased in tempo. Charging in turn at each of the four corner fires which illuminate the clearing, I shouted, 'Stay, stay, heathen'.

Then I rushed in among the dancers, disrupting their stately pattern. They ran hither and thither to avoid my groping hands. Jangamuttuk slowed the rhythm, and now the dancers began a stamping dance around me, coming closer and closer until they were pressing against me. They moved in and hid me from the sight of the audience. The rhythm changed again and they moved out. There was a mutter from the mainlander mob. I had vanished. Where I had been cowering under the onslaught was nothing but smooth earth. This clever finale my father had planned in advance. Before the dance he had ordered a pit to be dug, which was then roofed with boughs and bark and covered over with earth. A small opening had been left unstrengthened, through which I could wriggle while the dancers hid me from sight, which they then covered up. I stayed within the hole until the ceremony was over and the ground was deserted. I then emerged, filled in the pit so that no sign of it remained and slipped back to our mob.

The local blackfellows were impressed with our ceremony, though we knew that without didgeridoo players and with our lessened numbers it was but a pallid thing. Still, Waai was much taken with the ghost songs and wanted to give Jangamuttuk others in exchange. He said that as they had enjoyed our ceremony so much, his mob would stage a ceremony for us the next night. 'It is one which has come down from the north and is for everyone to see. In fact we were told to perform it often as it would help to alleviate what is happening up there,' he informed Jangamuttuk and then explained its importance. 'With it came the message that a catastrophe was happening in that the poles which hold up the sky were rotting and needed to be replaced. We were urged to send stone axes so that new poles could be fashioned. We sent these, but since then have heard nothing further and as the sky is still up there and has not fallen to crush us, this must mean that the poles have been replaced. But these are only the northern ones and I have wondered if the same thing is happening to the southern ones. It might be interesting to live under a tilted sky, but perhaps not. Are they still firmly standing?'

'As firmly as they can be in these times,' Jangamuttuk replied. 'I myself conducted some of the last ceremonies to keep them upright and hard as stone. They are like crags and should remain standing for a very long time. Our problem was different. A hole in the sky developed through which came a horde of ghosts. Our ceremony was to repair the damage and prevent more coming through. Still, it may have been too late and the hole may be becoming larger and larger, letting through the ghosts in countless multitudes.'

'The times are indeed rough,' Waai agreed, 'and we shamans must struggle to return it to its original smoothness. At least the poles remain upright down there where it is, I have heard, very cold. They must be frozen solid and as hard as stone, and thus free of rot and insects. It is not like that far to the north where the rain falls all summer long and termites build large camps covering acres of land. But it seems that the poles have been replaced and so this ceremony was very efficacious in driving away the inimical forces which threatened them.'

My father, the ritual master of our mob, was always eager to see and trade old ceremonies for new ones. He had collected in his mind hundreds of songs and rituals, and these songs I sing are from him. He taught them to me. His songlines were sung until he passed over, and it was then that I began to add verses of my own. So it is understandable that he was eager to add this one to his collection. 'It is right,' he said to Waai, 'that I receive this ceremony. When one enters a new land, one needs to be able to sound out its hidden rhythms and sing its melodies.'

'That is so,' Waai replied, 'though this one is not from here but, as I've said, comes from the far north where the seasons and vegetation are different and the land is not as it is here. We have our own and these can only be passed on to fellow shamans. There is one which ...' He broke off, looked at me and asked as if I was not there, 'And how is this boy? Is he ready yet, for there seems something about him?'

My father stared at me and shrugged. 'He is one of us, though perhaps too much a dreamer. He might lose himself if he is not careful. Still, he must make his own way and I can only lead him so far.'

'He may be ready to move on to these things.'

'Well, he tasted the blood of his first life today and it caused a fever. The spirit of an animal awakened in him, one that likes the taste of blood,' he replied, then shrugged again, dismissing me from his mind.

They sat in silence for a time, then Waai got up, gestured and went off into the darkness beyond the camp. Jangamuttuk ignored his departure for a while, before he too got to his feet. 'That Crowman needs an Eagleman with sharp eyes to lead him back to camp. Without me, he'll be lost in the darkness,' he said, and followed after Waai.

They had not returned by the time sleep claimed us, nor had they returned when I rose with the sun. The others went off to hunt with the local men while I decided to go to the beach and see how Wadawaka was doing. Over the few days on the land, our hunting had been very successful. We enjoyed ranging far and wide after the confines of the vessel and any fears we might have had of being in a strange place had been lessened by our connecting with the local mob who joined us in the hunt. We had supplied Wadawaka with a plentiful supply of meat to salt and pack away in barrels.

I found him hard at work, hammering on the lid of a cask. He finished this before acknowledging my presence. I looked away from his glance, for he had been left alone to do most of the necessary work, but this did not seem to perturb him overmuch as he merely commented, 'Ceremonies and dances might be all right when we have time, but to go on this is as important. There will come a time when we can't land and replenish our supplies. Ahead of us, there is this long stretch of coastline; it extends on and on with few landing places. The cliffs fall sheer into the ocean and beyond the land is bare and dry. No rivers flow into the sea and at one place where we shall land, we shall find sand dunes. Beyond them, within the bowels of the earth, is water, but that place is dangerous and we may be able to avoid it. If not, so be it, for on voyages there are many perils which must be overcome. There are many stories of Sinbad, Ulysses and others who did as we do.'

'Tell me some of these stories,' I demanded, thinking that he might know some of these voyagers, and also I was curious about how he could know what lay ahead. Had he voyaged along this coast before, perhaps with that Sinbad? He merely grunted as he returned to his work. I handed him the lid to another cask.

'Must get water aboard next, though we soon shall have another chance to replenish our supply,' he said. 'There is coming towards us a ship that will prove both dangerous and profitable to us. It is loaded with supplies which we need. There may be other ships coming this way too and it is best that we leave this place before they arrive. They see this schooner here and they come to find out who we are, for they claim all this land as theirs now. And it will not go well for us when they find black folk in command of a vessel. They feel that only they have the right to sail the seas and not us blackfellows. It will go hard with us too when they find out that the schooner is stolen. It will not be a flogging matter, but a hanging one.'

'You have been with them a long time and know their ways, but how do you know them now and in the future?' I demanded again. 'These local blackfellows could not have told you. They know nothing about the ghosts sailing along their shores. You have not seen the ghosts either, for we have not seen another ship since we sailed, and even though Father mentioned something he saw he often sees things that are not there. It's all gammon,' I ended querulously. I did not like the fact that my father and mother and now my friend Wadawaka had secrets I was not privy to.

Again he did not answer. Instead he busied himself with carrying a cask to the dinghy. I picked one up and helped him; I even rowed the laden boat to the schooner. As I leant on the oars, he suddenly asked me, 'What three exists where three are not?'

'I don't know,' I replied gruffly, for I was in a huff and annoyed at him.

'Well, I'll give you an answer to the riddle. It's like this,' he replied, ignoring my petulance. 'Ceremonies exist where there are workers; but ceremonies cannot exist when there is no one to prepare the ground. That's the first one, and from my land too. The second one is that grass exists where there are no animals to eat the grass; but there are no animals where there is no grass. And the last one is,' he concluded, 'water exists where there is no thing to drink it; but no thing can exist where no water is.'

'And what does this mean?' I asked, somewhat exasperated at his way of talking which was similar to how my father answered when he did not want to give a straight reply to one of my questions.

'Well, it means that if you get down and do your bit, you'll end up with something,' he replied with a shrug, as if to say anyone with a little common sense could see this.

I shipped my oars deftly and swung the dinghy against the side of the vessel. Wadawaka caught a trailing rope and made her fast. He passed the casks up to me on deck, then came aboard to stow them carefully below. As he did so, he seemed to hesitate and suddenly made a sign. 'There, that should fix them,' he muttered, then went on, 'Flowing water and darkness, the smell of earth and the creaking of timbers – what does it mean?' He said this to himself and I did not bother to answer him. I had had enough of riddles. We came up on deck and he secured the hatch covering, then loaded the dinghy with the empty water kegs. 'Far too few, but on the way we can pick up some more from that vessel travelling with a mist of doom about her.'

When the half-dozen water kegs were unloaded, we rested and Wadawaka, deeply troubled about something, again went on in riddles. 'You know,' he said, 'once, in my mother's country, there lived in a cave a woman who knew the future and could control the weather. She dressed all in blue cloth and lived only on castor oil from a plant with spiky fruit, one which I have not found down here. It is a medicine for the stomach when it is blocked up. Well, the women in the village took care of her, collected the seeds, pounded them, cooked them and took them to her cave. She was married – at least this is what was told to me by my mother – married to a big snake, a python, who lived in the forest and slithered to her cave at night. That snake entered into her and spoke to her in the dream state. That's how that woman knew everything and could bring the rain or stop it if she desired. She was what is called a witch, a *mangu*, but one night a flame appeared on the hilltop above her cave. It was a leopard with some powers of his own. He waited until that snake entered that woman and, when he did so, Leopard bounded down and swallowed them both up. Now Leopard, he had that woman in his belly and she had that snake in her belly. He was one in three. There were those two in him. Now he could dream the future from that snake and control the rain from that woman. That's how my mother told me it was, though I don't know about Leopard controlling the rain, but he can dream the future when he puts his mind to it and lets that snake come through to him.'

I nodded as if I understood and Wadawaka smiled sardonically. 'Come on, enough of stories, there are those kegs to fill.'

The spring was up from the beach and a short distance from the head of the track. We lugged the kegs up. It was a hard scramble in parts and we were tuckered out by the time we had them there. As we rested before filling them, I told Wadawaka about the previous night's ceremony and proudly described my part in it. 'And you know what,' I told him excitedly, 'that mob of blackfellows are going to put on one of theirs over the next few nights. Father's very excited and last night he went off with that Crow and hasn't returned yet. I wanted to go with them, but it's secret business they're about. I hope that I get to take part in it.'

'Yes, it will prove helpful to us during our voyage. Your father is the singer of songs and the performer of ceremonies. He knows much that is valuable, but not at this moment for there is the material as well as the spiritual and so let us finish off these barrels, eh? When the job is done, the singing and dancing begins in good heart, eh?'

We exchanged smiles and put our backs into our work. I tried to think over what Wadawaka had said, but felt too puzzled to continue. It was easier to do the work and get it over with so that we could corroboree.

CHAPTER THREE

That evening we found that the local mob had redone the ground, forming it into a circle at the quarters of which piles of wood had been stocked ready to be lit. They were camped close to the ground and their cooking fires smoked with the smell of kangaroo, possum and even one of those giant birds which they had trapped for us especially as they believed that it was the most worthy of repasts for guests.

'This is the father and mother of all birds. We call it Wakajee,' Waai told us as he began cutting up the plucked emu.

We eyed the monster fowl as he hacked off the feet at the knee joints and tossed them away, then opened up the belly, pulled out the guts and the rest of the insides and carefully placed them on a bed of leaves. These he flung into the fire where they sizzled as the flames died down. Before long there were only glowing coals and he used two twigs to pincer the guts out, then pushed the coals aside to get at two hot stones which he rolled into the cavity of the giant fowl. He tied the thighs to the neck then quickly dumped the carcase into the hole where the stones had been. He covered it with coals and ashes, then added some wood.

'Right, we'll just leave him to cook,' he informed us, 'and while that is being done we'll snack on these bits. They're the best part and I have reserved them as a special treat for you strangers who have never tasted such delicacies before.'

We watched him separate out the entrails and other parts on the bed of leaves. He pointed out different portions to the men who took them up gingerly. The women and I did not receive any and we stared hungrily as the entrails were chewed, apparently with relish. Waai was a finicky cook and kept poking a sharpened twig through the mound of ashes and into the carcase beneath. At last he deemed it done. He gave a grunt of approval and with the help of two sticks rolled the fowl out onto a large sheet of paperbark.

'There,' he exclaimed, 'done to perfection. Now if you'll just pass me one of your sharp knives which cut so much better than our stone ones, I'll do the honours.'

He cut the emu across the middle, carefully separating the upper and lower sections, then hacked off the two legs and the wings. Next he cut off the fat and removed the tailbone, the breast and the neck. He hacked off the head and tossed it away, then turned his attention and skill to the thighs. The meat was sliced off and the muscles pulled out. Only the bare bones were left. He left off his carving to point at the muscles.

'You see that big muscle there, we call it the old one and it is for the eldest among us. You,' he indicated Jangamuttuk. 'Now, each of the others have a name and each is for one of you mob. Now you'll see why we call it the mother and father of all birds. This one is plumed pigeon, that one the diamond dove, that small one the zebra finch. The boy can start on that for he is almost drooling. This one is willy wagtail and is for the eldest of the women. This one is painted finch and the other is redcapped robin.' And so he divided up the giant bird according to the species until he came to the heart. 'Now here is the heart and it is filled with that dark stuff, the cooked blood, and who do we give this to? He looks a bit pale,' he said indicating me, 'he needs some blood to darken him up,' and he tossed me the heart. I bit into it, tasting the curdled blood and sucking up the sweet juices. 'That'll put some colour into him,' Waai exclaimed, then fell to feasting with us.

Although I had approached the eating of the fowl with trepidation, I found that it tasted better than one of our mutton birds. We gorged ourselves on the dark bird meat and while we ate Waai explained the significance of the cycle of ceremonies which were to begin that evening. He informed us that as the poles which held up the sky had obviously been replaced, a secondary reason now came into being, which was to pacify the demon which was roaming the lands to the north and had threatened them in the first place. 'If we perform this ceremony correctly, he will not come this way. The songs will carry to him on the wind and will scare him off. Then, with the end of the ceremony, he will fall into a deep sleep and remain unconscious as long as we keep on performing the ceremonies at regular intervals. He has a name, *Moma*, and I have been told that he did much damage up there until the shamans dreamt this cycle of ceremonies. He has a hunger for fresh meat and blood, human meat and blood, and when he is overcome by this urge, he roams about hunting his prey. It is easy to recognise his tracks, for they are of a foot without toes and close together, for he is an ugly dwarf though immensely strong. In our ceremony we bind his feet to his legs so that he can only hobble. This slows him down so that our songs can catch him and put him down.'

'Feet without toes,' Jangamuttuk broke in, 'I know those tracks, they are made by ghosts who wear on their feet what they call boots. We know that devil all right! He roamed across our land and we could not stop him.'

'No wonder you had to flee from your island,' Waai exclaimed. 'You lacked this cycle of ceremonies and could not slow him down enough to put him to sleep. He roamed about eating your flesh and drinking your blood. How many of you must have ended up in his belly? If only you had had our ceremony ...'

'Yes, but I dreamt another ceremony, the one which we performed last night. This enabled us to escape from him.'

'It does have, I admit, a certain power, but nowhere near as much as this cycle does. You'll see for yourself soon, for now the sun is falling beneath the earth and it must start with the first darkness.'

Stuffed with meat, we arose somewhat slowly from our feasting and followed him to the *boro* circle where the large fires were lit. The women were already sitting at one side of the circle, across from a square shelter of boughs upon which sheets of bark had been tied and over which clumps of long grass had been attached in spiral patterns. Waai took us to sit in front of the women, along with those local men who were not to dance that night. Darkness descended and more branches were flung onto the fires. They blazed up to illuminate the dance ground. Waai and the performers went into the hut. We sat and waited for the ceremony to begin.

Waai emerged from the shelter in his costume. Two long red bands gleamed wetly across his forehead and down both sides of his face, neck and body to end on his thighs. He was wearing bark amulets to which had been fastened tufts of crow feathers, and into his hair grass had been plaited so that now it was indeed a tuft of grass. His human hair belt also had been decorated with crow feathers which hung down on either side of his pubic covering of pearl shell, similar to our own though the designs were different. His ankles and the lower parts of his legs were wrapped around with leggings made from paperbark bound with twigs with the leaves still on them. He lifted each leg in turn and singed them over a small fire which had been kindled directly in front of the hut. As he stepped away, I saw that the red bands glowed with a phosphorescent greenish-white outline, onto which patches of dark crow down had been stuck, glued on, as I learnt later, with dried crow blood. Waai turned to the hut and pulled from the wall a short stick forked with sharpened kangaroo femur bones. He gestured with this at the door of the shelter and some men came out and sat in front of us. They began clapping together curved boards which gave out a sharper sound than our clapsticks. These, I later learnt, were called *makee* and were sometimes used to bring down birds in flight as they had a curious property of returning to their owners if flung into the wind. I later learnt this art and made use of it on an occasion when danger threatened, but that is another story.

The men, in time to their clacking, sang, *'Walla koorpana kooloo waroo.'*

Waai shook his stick vigorously in their direction and sang back, *'Meun korunna linja rooeri. Meun korunna weat yorinni.'*

He stamped his left foot, then his right, then ducked down into a half squat and in time to the rhythm and singing vibrated his knees and thighs. He sprang upright and began stamping out a dance while vibrating the muscles of his thighs. Other men emerged from the hut and took up the stamping dance. The sitting men struck their *makee* and sang on in a high keening fashion. The women took up the song, adding to the rhythm a flatter sound by clapping their hands on the vee of their thighs so that it gained in thickness. The singing continued throughout the night and the dancers took turns to perform. When the light of dawn softened the darkness and the sun awoke at his camp beneath the horizon and poked up his head into the cloudy sky, a breeze came from the ocean to rustle the trees. Suddenly there was a gale of wild laughter from a huge gum tree. It was as if the *Moma* had alighted there and laughed at our efforts to dispel him. The laughter mocked the clacking of the two *makee* which Waai beat fiercely together as he whirled about in a dance, bobbing his head close to the earth and rising it up again, as a bird searching for seeds. A magpie chortled and the laughter stopped as a flock of crows settled into the tree. Their coming marked the end of the first night's ceremony.

In the early morning light we straggled back to the camp to sleep the day away, then awake and feast until the sun writhed over the horizon again. His campfire was streaking red into the sky as we trooped to the ceremonial ground. Darkness arrived and our fires blazed forth. Waai began the performance as on the previous evening, but he had changed his costume for this night. In the centre of his forehead a third eye was painted, red and glaring. It even seemed to wink as he wrinkled his forehead and bobbed his head in the dance. This evening he held and postured with a short length of tightly rolled kangaroo skin wound tightly about with string. It contained his medicine which energised the ceremony. He dispensed with this after showing it to the dancers and the audience, then took up bunches of herbs in his hands. He passed these over the central fire until they smouldered and then, in a high-stepping dance, came towards us and waved the bunches over us so that the pungent smoke wrinkled our nostrils. He was right in front of me. I stared and saw that his face was covered in white down, except for the lips which seemed to be smeared with blood. As the night progressed the dancing became wilder and wilder and the dancers worked themselves into a frenzy, driven even higher by the staccato rhythm which the men and women kept up until dawn began to recover the bush from the claws of the night. The rhythm slowed and stopped. Only Waai continued it, striking his two *makee* together and dragging his feet along the ground in time to the clacking. Then there came from the undergrowth the call of a bird, 'buk-buk, buk-buk,' which set up a separate rhythm of its own. A crow cawed in response, and Waai stopped his dance as the sun streaked the bush with light to put to flight the devil which had been evoked.

The third night seemed an anticlimax and the sleepless nights and fitful rest during the day were beginning to have their effect on us. During the ceremony some of us, including myself, dozed off, moving in and out of consciousness. On one occasion, I came to to see Waai dancing in front of me. He wore on his head something resembling a dark stovepipe hat and across his forehead had been painted two white parallel lines a few inches apart with the space between filled with red. His body was decorated with a crosshatching of thin white lines and he wore leggings of bark decorated with patches of white and black down in circular designs. The scene and details were as vivid and intense as a dream. In a somnolent state, I watched him as he held these over the fire until they caught alight. He danced vigorously with sparks flashing out from his leggings. He tugged from the wall of the hut a piece of wood shaped like a musket. There were white cockatoo feathers tied to the muzzle. He gestured with the feathered end at the door of the hut. A second figure emerged, similarly painted. It was Jangamuttuk, my father. He came level with Waai and both began the high-stepping stamping dance, waving their sticks threateningly towards us. Now they stamped vigorously, quivering their thigh muscles as they danced towards us. Those men and women who were awake lessened the rhythm in an effort to slow them, but all this did was to create a more complex syncopation. A group of dancers emerged from the hut to join them. They faced us in a line, spreading their legs apart and quivering their muscles while they jabbed the feathered ends of their staffs at us. I jerked fully awake as from the bush came the sobbing scream of someone in agony. The scream continued on and on, falling and rising again and again, then from beneath it there came a stuttering whirling susurration which steadily rose until it drowned out the screaming. Then, abruptly, all fell into silence before a crow cawed as it lifted from the tree.

Dawn arrived to brighten the bush and dissipate our mood. We gave a collective sigh of relief which turned into a groan as clouds rushed in to overcome the sun. The light and the colours leached back towards the night. The dancers suddenly gave a shout and rushed to the shelter. They stabbed again and again at its walls and attempted to pull it down. They failed, and with this the night's ceremony ended. A light drizzle began to fall which strengthened into a downpour. It drove us back to camp where we rendered the bark huts in which we were sleeping somewhat waterproof. It was a mournful, unrestful day. We tried to sleep in the huts, but the rain seeped in and, worse, the weather turned chilly. Even when sleep came it was a fitful napping filled with strange dreams in which I was pursued by shadows whose only substance was claws and fangs.

'Pilil aroola wotya rum brina,' began the fourth night's performance. We were damp and miserable in mind and body. The fires glowed fitfully, emitting clouds of smoke, and the bush pressed in on us. The clack-clack of the *makee* sounded sodden and the women's cupped hands thudded into their groins to produce a sombre note. Jangamuttuk and Waai, both decorated similarly to the patterns of our own Ghost Dreaming but with the fiery third eye painted on their foreheads, danced listlessly as if something was sapping their strength. Both held staffs shaped like muskets, but the thinner ends were pointed spear tips. They marched around the clearing, pointing with their sticks and weakly calling to the men in the audience to join them. A few got to their feet to shuffle forward, among them some of our mob. I felt too tired to do so and remained seated, hunched over from the cold. Despair spread over the boro ground. It seemed that the Moma lurked in the dripping darkness ready to pounce. The clouds sank lower and threatened more rain. A wind laden with sea smell blew and darted the flames and smoke of the fires this way and that. Suddenly there came an explosion of thunder. The dancers hesitated. The rhythm fell away, then began again weakly until those of the dancers holding *makee* held them high and began a furious rhythm, as if trying to frighten away the thunder spirit. Now they danced in one spot raising their legs high and bringing them down with a thud. Crack-crack, clack-clack, the dancers stamped frantically to a rhythm which threatened to join together in one long peal of sound. The women thudded along with their cupped hands and lessened the rhythm a little. The inertia was gone now, along with my tiredness. I wanted to leap up and join in, but when I tensed my body to do so a man of the local mob sitting next to me pressed me down. Suddenly the thunder spirit struck again, a single peal of thunder which now, instead of overawing dancers and musicians, seemed only to add to the wildness. Again the thunder spirit struck his axe and then from the scowling darkness came a whirling sound which rose higher and higher. It became a shriek as from the bush a figure entered the arena in a series of leaps. The thunder spirit struck sparks and in the distance there was the drumming sound of rain. Blue flame flashed down from the sky to touch the top of the tall gum tree and then run down its side into the earth. My father and Waai flung their spears at the figure who casually brushed them aside. Now his leaps gave way to a crippled hobble, but not for long – he leapt high and spread his legs wide. The cords which had been binding his legs snapped and he was free.

The devil danced towards the audience and stopped directly in front of me, his thighs jerking with his dancing. I saw that his penis was erect and had pushed up his pubic covering so that it rested on it. Now he grasped his rigid member in his hand and threatened the women with it. I looked away and up at his face. It had been painted stark white except for the fanged mouth which had been daubed with red ochre, or was it blood? This dripped in great gobs from his mouth. I shrank back as the face came down to me. The devil squatted and danced on his haunches, then leapt into the air and turned his back and moved away. On his back was a framework of sticks over which a membrane had been stretched. As he pranced away, he moved the muscles of his shoulders so that they fluttered and spread as if they were wings. He approached the men who threatened him with whatever they held in their hands. Contemptuously he clasped his penis and lifted it towards them before darting among them, snatching at their boomerangs and sticks and flinging them into the hut. He came to the central fire and picked up two brands and whirled them over his head until they blazed. He danced with them for a time, then tossed one at the dancers and the other at the audience. He took up two more, whirled them around his head and flung them into the hut. They blazed inside, then the bark caught and the whole structure burst into flame. A wailing came from everyone. I also wailed until I noticed that there was something familiar about this devil. I stared as he danced with Jangamuttuk and Waai towards me. They stopped directly in front of where I was sitting and then, with a shriek, the devil fell on me. I struggled beneath him as, almost at the same instant, thunder exploded. It deafened me, and lightning followed to blind me. A howling wind rushed in with a cascade of rain while in utter terror I fought to escape from the devil. The weight of his body held me down. I was in a panic which increased as I felt him shift, letting other hands hold me. These lifted me up. Held high, I was raced from the clearing. Something bitter was thrust into my mouth and pushed down my throat until I had to swallow. I was flung into a sack and felt myself being carried away before darkness claimed my senses.

CHAPTER FOUR

'See this, it is a message stick. I have carved it for you.' Waai's voice broke into my darkness and lifted me into a dim awareness. 'When you continue your voyage west and land and meet other mobs, you must show it to them. It belongs to the Crow division and will serve as an introduction to those of our kin. You will be welcomed instead of speared.' His laughter echoed in my aching head.

'But will it do for us who are of the Eaglehawk division?' replied Jangamuttuk. 'I know those Crows and they are not to be trusted. There is that little matter of your ancestor stealing our women, and that was only one of his tricks. Perhaps this is more of the same thing.'

Crow broke into a laugh again. 'No. See, here I have carved the symbol for Crow and another for Eaglehawk and these wavy lines show that we have a close relationship, not kin but very close to it. These circles within that boundary represent my country. Here is the coastline and there is your direction of travel. Lastly, this mark is my personal signature. Anyway, it is up to you whether you use it or not. The stick is merely physical and there are shamans along the way who will contact you psychically and thus know you.'

'Or destroy me. Some shamans are evil and may cast a spell on me.'

'Sing you while pointing the bone, eh? Well, you must take your chances and be alert. My message stick will open communications, but remember not to play the great sorcerer. Though that would be difficult when your rituals seem to be to some extent undeveloped. Not even in our old stories do any of us ride on our Dreaming animals. Can you, if you have heard it, recall the story about Eaglehawk and Crow ...? Ah, our boy has returned into his mind though not his body and perhaps he would like to hear it.'

Jangamuttuk replied in a huff, 'I know the complete cycle of those stories including the one when Crow became as black as night owing to his misdeeds. Eaglehawk is the source of my magic and when Crow thought he had him safely trapped in a cave, he became a centipede and made his escape by winding his way through the gaps between the rocks with which Crow had sealed the entrance.'

'That's the one. There are others which are secret. Ones in which shamans learn to become animals, but never to merely ride them. Perhaps we should perform the ritual and see if such a complete transformation can be effected on you even though you belong to the Eagle division.'

Another and deeper voice cut in, it was Wadawaka. 'But what about this one here? When the fruit is ripe, it needs to be eaten, otherwise it becomes rotten.'

Waai rejoined, 'He's just a boy and unimportant. Let him lie, he is dumb and blind like a dead man.'

Wadawaka: 'Like a zombie. He can hear, but cannot speak. He can even move if needs be, but not on his own account. At least this is what I have heard, though I have never seen one of these walking dead.'

Waai: 'A what?'

Wadawaka: 'A zombie, *obeah* man, that is, a *maban* or shaman in my language. They have strong magic and can make the dead walk again.'

Jangamuttuk: 'That may be, but this young one is not dead. He has only had too much of that *pitchuri* Waai stuffed in his mouth. It is his first time and there might be bad results. Was it a necessary part of the ceremony to kidnap him? Why not one of your own?'

Waai: 'All the good roles we reserved for you, our guests. It is our way of showing hospitality. It will give a dramatic finale to the ceremony in which all can participate. Later, when he comes to, though he will be groggy we will take him back to the *boro* ground and declare that we have fought and vanquished *Moma,* thus saving this boy from having his flesh eaten and his blood drunk. There will then be much rejoicing, but this will be after midnight and so we have plenty of time to prepare for our entrance which must be at dawn. Now the whole mob are in mourning and a funeral service is about to be performed. After this, just before the spirit is sent on his way, we will intervene to reveal that he is still alive and well.'

Wadawaka: 'And that will be the end of the ceremony. It has to be, for we have tarried here too long. Our vessel is ready to sail and there is a place further along the coast to which we must go. The time is nigh and we need to be there to get the things we need, things which are hard to get in this land. It is said that when all the food is eaten, the guest departs and so, with the ceremony over, we will be on our way.'

Waai: 'Yes, I know you wish to be off and that is why I have given Jangamuttuk his message stick tonight. When day breaks you are free to go without misgivings, though you might be tired.'

Wadawaka: 'We will sail with the outgoing tide in the afternoon. Thus we will have time to rest, and when the sails are set there is little to do for most of us.'

Jangamuttuk: 'Enough of tomorrow. Crow has mentioned that which I wish to see and participate in. There is time to do it before we spread our sails. Crow, I am ready!'

Waai: 'Impatience is not a virtue, it only indicates an impetuosity of thought, but indeed it is the time for you to undertake the ritual. Perhaps it is the only time, for this is one of the few places where it can be done. Now, let me build up the fire and ... Where is my medicine bag? There are herbs in it I need. Ah, there it is, next to the comatose boy. *Moma* still has him in his grip. Well, this is not for him. You know, this place is powerful in magic. It is where the rainbow snake came to rest and left his scales behind. You see them gleaming in the walls. A strong place to conduct the ritual, for there are three things necessary for its success: knowledge of the songs and ritual, a shaman with the ability to perform them and the proper place to conduct them. You are fortunate, for who knows when you will find such a place again, or for that matter a man of my talents and knowledge.'

The conversation had drifted into my head without any effort at hearing on my part. I could not understand much about which they spoke, but felt relieved that my kidnapping had been part of the ceremony, and an important part too. I would have smiled, except that my body was paralysed and no matter how hard I tried I could not move a muscle, except for those of my eyelids. They creaked up, and although I could not move my head, my eyes were alive and I could shift them about to examine much of the place where they had taken me. A chanting in a language I did not know began as I let sight impressions enter my eyes. I became lost in the rocky wall of the cave. The fire flickered on it, evoking mites of light which activated the rods of my eyes so that I could feel them individually. I lost any consciousness of sounds and even the sharp crack-crack of clapsticks did not arouse me from my contemplation.

Acute feelings began to return to my body. I felt the individual grains of sand on which I lay. I watched the slow-growing stalagmites and stalactites reach from floor and ceiling to join in columns which warped the space I existed in. The flames danced and flickered in the darkness and tiny specks of mitre spun from the walls to touch my eyeballs. A strong draught from the deeper reaches of the cave agitated the cells of my skin, moving across me towards where the open night lay waiting for the dawn and my liberation. It struck the flames and twisted them until indistinct figures formed at the extreme of my vision. There was Jangamuttuk, but beside him was a huge goanna; and by Wadawaka snarled a strange spotted creature similar to the marsupial tiger. In front of them a giant crow squawked as he lifted one claw to scatter some darkish powder onto the flames. They turned a rainbow hue. I felt a wrenching at my stomach as if my intestines were seeking to escape through my mouth. I was still paralysed, but my body writhed internally.

I tried to call out, but my throat was numb. Specks of light floated from the walls and descended over my face. I breathed them in. Sharp pains racked my chest. I wanted to gulp in great volumes of air, I wanted to vomit out what was twisting inside me. I could do neither and then, in my sight, I saw Jangamuttuk and the goanna merge and then Wadawaka and his creature. Now there were only the crow, the goanna and the spotted creature there. They spoke in my head.

Crow: 'There, it is done. You were halfway there already. You can even learn how to shapeshift into other forms.'

Goanna: 'I am at home in this body, so why should I desire to be some other animal? Goanna was a friend and now he is part of me as I am part of him, but before we supplemented each other and I could hold my crystal weapon and play my clapsticks. Now I have only legs. How do I do that now?'

Crow: 'You have a mouth, don't you, and those things of our trade are safely stored in our stomachs. When one is needed, simply regurgitate it and hold it there.'

The Spotted Creature: 'I feel the need to test myself out in the night sky and across the darkened land – but what is happening to the boy?'

Crow: 'What could happen to him? He is here only to be taken back when the time comes.'

The Spotted Creature: 'But when the fruit is ripe, it falls. Look!'

Movement returned to my body, but without my control. I twisted and writhed on the cave floor. My insides sought to push out through my skin and my skin was seething with disquiet. Then my bones began to melt and reform. My face broke apart and came together again, but not as it had been. I opened my mouth wide to scream out my terror and a tongue flopped out. I tried to leap to my feet to escape the agony, but could not. I tried to pull myself up with my hands, but I had none – only paws. I gazed down to find that I had a hairy animal body. I gave a yelp of terror and churned my legs. On all fours, I stumbled and tripped over, then through sheer instinct, managed to run towards the mouth of the cave. I smelt the fresh air of the open bush, but my legs became entangled and I rolled the last few feet to the mouth of the cave and over a ledge. Now I was falling down what appeared to be a sheer cliff. I gave a yelp and churned my legs. Suddenly I found myself rising in the air. It seemed impossible, but I was flying. How or why, I did not know then, or even what had happened to me.

Suddenly the whole world churned as my stomach cramped. The very landscape lurched and changed and where the dark fastnesses of the bush had been, now streaks of light angled from the horizon towards a huge central blaze of light. Strange and pungent odours came to my nostrils and my eyes stared down at what I did not know. As quickly as I had found it, I lost the art of flying and began to fall towards a streak of light which resolved into countless twin dots of light rushing towards and away from that central blaze of light. As I fell closer it itself became millions of illuminated dots, moving and unmoving, blinking and unblinking. My eyes watered from rank gases, my ears filled with raucous sounds, and my mind filled with terror. I had only one desire – to be away from this awful place which could only be the skyworld. I thought that I had died and was approaching the campfires of all those who had gone before. I gave a whimper and fled to the darkest patch I could find. Again there came that churning. The sights, sounds and smells vanished as suddenly as they had appeared. The skyworld was replaced by my friendly environment. Familiar stars shone down on me and below me was the bush and the fires of the ceremonial ground, and just beyond the campfires glowing softly in the darkness. I wished to land there, but then the scent of humans filled my nostrils and with the scent came mistrust. I trotted in flight over the camp and away into the friendly darkness of the bush.

I do not know how long I flew over the darkened bushscape. It stretched on and on as infinitely as the sky, and I flew on and on without effort. At last a growing thirst wished me towards a line of winding trees underneath which I smelt water. I flew along their winding length and then the gleam of a billabong drew me down to the ground. I had but to wish and one moment I was flying, the next my feet were on the ground. Moving across the ground seemed to be more difficult than going through the air. I stumbled as I touched solid earth. To get my four legs working in unison took an ability which I consciously lacked, but I found that if I let this new body of mine operate on its own, it managed better than under the direction of my mind. And I discovered that I had other things to marvel out rather than concentrating on walking on four legs. My sight extended at both sides so that I could see more of ... Well, there wasn't much to see, only darkness. My hearing was acute and better suited to the night than my eyes. It detected the slightest rustle, identifying the different animals from the sounds they made. I felt the urge to hunt and imagined tearing apart my prey. My nostrils quivered as they separated out the animals' odours, but underlying all the perfumes of these living things were the rich loamy scent of the earth and the delicious sweetness of the water. My jaws dripped with saliva as I came to the muddy bank of the pool and lowered my snout to lap at the water. It had never tasted so good. It was like drinking an elixir pungent with the colorations of my newly acute senses of taste and smell. At last, satisfied, I lifted my head and licked my chops. Now would come the feeding. My ears pricked at the slight rustle of a possum, my nostrils quivered at its scent. I traced its passage through the trees as it came towards the pool. Soon it would descend to drink and encounter my snapping jaws. I drooled at the thought.

It was then that my ears caught another sound that alerted me into stillness, a shook-shook sound that stopped at a tree. There was a squeal from the possum and the sound of rustling. My nostrils caught the smell of blood, rich and pungent, and beneath this a rankness that prickled the hair along my back. Suddenly there was a thud. My nose identified it as the possum falling from the tree. Low to the ground, I crept forward and came upon the body. I sniffed at the animal and at its ripped throat. I tasted the few drops of blood there and might have begun eating, but suddenly a dark shape fell from the tree and fastened on my neck. I gave a howl of terror and whirled, then rolled over and over trying to dislodge the thing from my throat. I snapped at it and my teeth fastened on a part of its body. Suddenly I was free and in the air, fleeing from the thing which now pursued me. Behind me came the steady shook-shook of wings. I rose higher and so did it. I swooped down among the trees and it followed and drew nearer. I smelt the rankness of stale blood and rotting flesh, which attracted me as much as it repelled. Still, I knew that it was dangerous. I had to escape to a safe place and set about doing something about my wound. My neck stung and I could not reach the spot with my tongue. It itched as if a poison had been injected into me. Perhaps I could roll in the mud and relieve it, but not while the thing was after me. I could taste the bitterness of its blood on my snout and smell the putrid smell of rotten meat which almost made me lure it down to the ground so that I might attack it. If I had not been new to my transformation and had been able to identify the creature, I might have turned and become the pursuer, but then all was new and strange to me. Instinctively, all I wanted was to go to ground and hide, but with that thing on my tail I could not. Instead I charged up into the sky, fleeing towards the only place of safety I knew.

The iodine smell of the sea drew me to it. From a distance my ears caught the sound of waves lapping at the land, I even heard the rough drag of sand being drawn away into the waters. There was the scuttling sound of a crab and then I was over the ceremonial ground with its massed clash of boomerangs, the words of a song and the stamp of human feet. As I flew over it, from one side rose a huge goanna, then a giant crow, its blackness almost lost in the darkness but I could identify it by smell, and lastly another creature with a strange shape and strange smell, though familiar. Still I did not hesitate, but rushed on ever faster. I reached the coastline and saw the schooner at anchor. There another creature rose to come towards me. It smelt of the sea mingled with another scent which I identified with relief as that of my mother, a human. But then, I was human too. But from behind me still came the shook-shook of those leathern wings and a hissing which made me flee out to sea. I was followed by the five other creatures.

Four gained on me, and from them came a feeling of reassurance. My fright left me as I identified the scents of Wadawaka and Jangamuttuk. I slowed as I recognised them and glanced back to see what had pursued me with the shook-shook of leathern wings. It was then that I saw Ludjee, my mother – who, unlike the others, rode her creature – draw level with the creature. She held something up and from it came a flash of red light. It revealed to me the shape of a giant bat. The ray of light from the crystal struck the bat's wing and passed through. The wing collapsed and the creature tumbled towards the ocean. The spume of a wave flung it up and somehow it recovered the use of its wing. Avoiding another of my mother's rays, it sped out to sea, towards the dark shape of a ghost ship ploughing steadily through the ocean waves at full sail. It was filled with the ghost smell which showed that many were aboard, though there was again a strong scent of blood and rotten meat. The bat swooped down to the ship and disappeared between its sails. I circled with the others, wondering if they would land on the ship. Ludjee came next to me on her creature, a giant manta ray, and ordered me in my mind to return to the beach. Goanna and the spotted creature, Leopard as it was named, backed up her demand.

We were all turning away from the vessel when suddenly there flashed into the sky, perhaps from the ship though later we couldn't be sure, a great beast with white fur and slavering jaws. It darted at Ludjee and with a blow from one of its huge paws knocked her off her manta ray and into the ocean. She disappeared under the surface, but her dreaming animal, Manta Ray, dived after her. Leopard turned with a snarl and leapt at the animal. With an answering snarl, it met his attack. They tumbled across the sky, tangled together. Goanna, now holding a glowing crystal in his mouth, fired a red ray wide of the two in an effort to distract the beast. Crow screeched a long screech, fluttered about the combatants and entered the fray. A large paw swiped at him and he turned and fled for the shore. A dark shape rose from the ship, then sank back as one wing gave out. I watched all this in utter amazement, for it was beyond anything I had experienced. Suddenly Leopard broke free of what he later told me was a giant white bear and Jangamuttuk seized the opportunity.

A ray from his crystal leapt out and struck the bear across the chest. A shout sounded in my head. The ray had burnt away all the fur leaving a black mark and blistered skin. The bear roared in fury, then fled into the night away from the ship and out to sea. Leopard and Goanna came after it, their crystals emitting red rays which the bear dodged before it outstripped their pursuit. They abandoned the chase and came back just as Ludjee, riding Manta Ray, emerged from the water and joined us. They talked in my head as we retreated to the land.

Ludjee: 'What have you done to my son? He wasn't ready for such a thing. How could you do it when there are such enemies about?'

Jangamuttuk: 'It was not my doing. I listened to that Crow and his three things that came together. Well, there were three things: a drug, a wily crow and his trickery. I should have known that a crow cannot change his colour. Still, he was as much surprised as I was when the boy transformed.'

Wadawaka: 'The fruit was ripe and now it has fallen. He must learn how to control himself now. What is he – some sort of dog?'

Jangamuttuk: 'A dingo they call them here, and it too is wily like Crow. Wily and wild. Look at him, like father like son. At least we both have four legs.'

Ludjee: 'It's no laughing matter, but as it's happened, I suppose it had to. And what happened to you two? Now you're all your animal. How can you play your clapsticks, Jangamuttuk, and how can you sound your *abeng*, Wadawaka? Do you think it is for the better to be as you now are?'

Jangamuttuk: 'I said that Crow tricked us. He made us over. But in some ways it is better.'

Wadawaka: 'Perhaps. I do feel more attuned to what I am. As a blackfellow cannot change the colour of his skin so a leopard cannot change his spots. One as the other, we are as we are for better or worse.'

Ludjee: 'Well, let us get back to land. Follow me for it is just about dawn.'

And she turned and with a blast from her conch shell summoned us to follow. I was getting used to my new shape and felt glad that I was as one of them now and privy to their secrets, but where the bat had bitten me still itched and I still tasted her blood in my mouth. This seemed to have infected me with another change. Even after they had shown me how to turn back into my human form, both feelings endured. There came also another effect. My mind at times seemed to be thinking another's thoughts. I even dreamt of a woman, a ghost woman with flowing yellow hair, but when I told Jangamuttuk and later Wadawaka about this, they both laughed and said that it was natural, and that if the urge had come sooner I could have satisfied it with one of the local girls who they had found not adverse to a bit of the strange. I shrugged at this and did not tell them of the phantom lap of waves or of seeing in a dim darkness unspeakable acts in which the tart taste of blood filled my mouth and flowed down my throat. I kept such things to myself, for Father explained away the unexplainable as the trickery of Crow and the aftereffects of his ceremony of transformation.

'There is always some disorientation,' he explained. 'And Crow changed you too quickly and without instruction. Sometimes it can cause a man to remain silly in the head, but you are not. In time you'll get used to it.'

I nodded at this while hearing in my head the shook-shook of leathern wings as a bat flew through the air, exulting as she sped to the hunt.

CHAPTER FIVE

Once, how long ago it seems, I was Amelia Fraser and I had a sister, Eliza. Now that life is finished with and I have entered into some other, far different state of existence. I am something else, and perhaps it is better than what I would have become. Before I was as other girls. Now I am perhaps far worse than females such as my sister Eliza who ended up marrying a sea captain, a man who proved to be the means by which I was enabled to take passage on this vessel aptly named the *Kore*. It was not an easy thing for me to do for I need my earth to support me, but perhaps when I have learnt to fully master my present state this dependence will lessen, though I am loath to try when the strength of its dominance might result not in my death, but in my ceasing to be. Such thoughts as these I have when I set about my feeding, slaking my hunger with the variations he taught me. At times, the desires he instilled in me are as strong as my need for sustenance and it is then that I do this, though I am and intend to remain a virgin until ... well, until the day of my ceasing, if that should ever occur, for I am careful and know I must be even more careful at those times when my thirst strikes me with such an overpowering force that rational thought is threatened and I drift in thought rather than think.

This is what occurred last night when, tired of the confines of the ship, I transformed, took wing and skimmed over the sea, exulting in the thrust of my wings, exulting in my freedom of flight which took me beyond all care. I reached the coastline and continued on inland. I saw the fires of the local people, naked and unashamed savages, and flew on until I landed to sample the blood of the strange fauna. I did so with a minimum of effort which left me dissatisfied, so I turned my attention on a sly young dog who savaged me when I struck. Blind with rage I pursued him, drawing out the chase as I fed on the terror in his mind. I was insensate in my play and did not detect the approach of creatures much like myself, neither human nor non-human, but they were without my thirst until I, in turn, became the pursued. I fled over the waters towards my haven which was the *Kore*. They followed eagerly and one of them, a human mounted on a strange sea creature – or was she a mermaid? – used a red light to sear my wing. I managed to recover and reached the ship, fluttering down to the deck. They were about to follow when a giant polar bear – yes, but again human and animal – rose to attack them. It was wild with a blood lust that rivalled my own, but it was not defending me. He rose to rend them apart. I identified him as a werebear and knew then that when I reach the new land I must be careful, for he and I can have no communion, being deadly rivals. The new land, yes, and now it fills my senses as the blood that the young dog took from me does its work, and I dream his dream, not as a dog but as a human. How strange it is for little Amelia Fraser to dream strong male dreams, and to know that he is sharing mine even as I participate in my snack before the rich red banquet, feeling its pulsating as I kneel and, in the attitude of prayer, gulp down the white blood that I have grown accustomed to.

These sailors, however, lack the staying power which would allow me to linger over my repast. Months at sea have filled them up and though the supply is copious and rich, it lacks the froth which prolonged milking gives it. This is the case again and although I lap up the white blood avidly I am still disappointed. A returning panic in my prey gives it some strength to struggle. I keep my eyes glued to his, hypnotising him so that he cannot move, throw me off or shriek out, though he is the last and there is no one to come to his aid. Now I pull myself up the length of his body and brush my tangled blonde hair from my face. How long since it has felt the brush and comb? I find the pulsing neck vein and sink my fangs in. His body gives a start and trembles as I draw forth his blood. I linger over my meal as I remember my own trembling when I had my first blooding. I sup and my mind drifts away.

In London we were poor, not as poor as poor, but my father was a wretched law clerk who mulled over depositions for a pitiful wage in the Law Serjeant's Inn. His subservience stopped at day's end when he came home to tyrannise us, his two daughters, and our mother, a colourless woman who had had all the spunk driven out of her long ago by his cruelty, though I never saw him use his fists on her. He believed that he was a gentleman fallen on hard times and this prevented him, I suppose. Poor mother, who only wanted to see us safely married and in such a relationship as she was suffocating in. Eliza was compliant to her wishes and so was I to a fashion, for at seventeen what else could I aspire to? I did have my small pleasures then, and these I managed to turn to a profit which supplemented the family income. I had discovered that I had a gift for rendering images onto cards, that is to draw and colour was my skill and my figures were the first to render faithfully those languorous females which, since they are now the subject of a masculine art, have become popular in the Royal Academy. I have never been to see them, but I have been told that their renderings are similar to my own and it is not a subject about which a person would lie.

At the end of the street, not where the market garden was and where our street of tiny but decent dwellings petered out into a dismal fogginess of countryside, but the eastern end where the road leading to the heart of the city throbbed with omnibuses, there stood an art emporium where I bought my instruments of drawing and colouring, although this was only occasionally as we too often lacked the necessary pence. Once, when I went there with my sister and was looking at the various pencils and colours, the proprietor came to me and asked what I wanted. He was quite rude and abrupt. I mentioned that I was an illustrator of cards and, as I had brought my satchel along, opened it and displayed my work. These, as I have said, depicted women and girls in attitudes of repose. There was one I liked especially. It was of a satyr hiding behind a stylised tree, gazing upon the fully draped form of a girl of about my own age who lay asleep and spread out before his lascivious gaze. The proprietor cast an eye over my work, then examined some of the sketches carefully. Finally he bought four of the cards for sixpence which I immediately spent on the tools of my art. As he was wrapping up my purchases he commented on my sketches and said that they would sell better if the female form was displayed to better advantage. 'A hint of ...' he insinuated, cupping his hands over his chest, then making a motion to curve out hips. 'It must not be vulgar but decorous, for I will have no indecencies in my emporium, but it will add to the attraction.' He smirked and said, 'Perhaps you should use a model such as your sister who has a nice form, or even your own, though that might be difficult.' He hurriedly ended the conversation, as if he were suggesting something not quite proper to we young ladies, with, 'They must be fully draped, of course, though ...'

And so, even though a young woman, I had a small income which gave me visions of an independence that made me eschew with some degree of spirit the constant talk of marriage which mother engaged in and which Eliza listened to, and which caused her to dream of a fine husband, perhaps even of Beau Brummel. On some afternoons, when she lay on her bed engaged in such imaginings, I took the advice of the proprietor and made her an inspiration for my illustrations. Although on occasion her pose was somewhat indecorous, especially when sleep claimed her, my swift sketches did away with such ungainliness. She was unaware of the uses I made of her and even when the captain appeared in her life and his uniform made an impression on her unformed mind, her dreams of wedded bliss added to the lustre I imparted to my figures.

One day, towards the evening but not too late to involve the censure of neighbours, I sallied forth, accompanied by Eliza, to the emporium with my latest series of cards. The proprietor bought them all and even complimented me on them. I was overjoyed for the sixpences had turned into shillings, and perhaps I lingered too long over their display for at last, on heeding my sister's imploring, when we emerged onto the road it was much later than I had thought, almost time for the lamplighter to make his rounds. The shadows of an early night were deepening all around us.

'We must hurry for father will be home soon,' Eliza said, tugging me along.

It was then that I became aware of a figure in the shadows of a building: a male form. I began to tremble as I darted a glance which struck his eyes. They glowed an eerie red, piercing my soul with a fire which was cool rather than overheated.

'Hurry, it is unseemly for us to be out at night,' Eliza urged, tugging again at my reluctant form.

In spite of her imploring, I hung back. Again my eyes reached out for that burning gaze before I allowed myself to be pulled away.

We crossed to our street and indeed it was late for the lamplighter was now making his rounds, but the orange flames of the street lamps made the dark more concealing than revealing what might be hidden there. Though nothing was for, as we turned into our street, he was beside me.

'So you are the young lady who gives shape to those marvellous females,' he said in a rich educated voice with a lingering foreign accent.

'Come away,' Eliza urged. 'Come away.'

But the man was obviously a gentleman. His clothes were well cut and a rich dark cape flowed from his shoulders. If only his eyes weren't so unsettling. I hurried along with my sister, but he kept pace.

'Perhaps, though I might be asking too much, you will allow me to see your cards before you sell them to that art emporium. I am a collector of sorts and, well, if all are as fine as your previous ones, I might commission you to do a series for me.'

'Sir, we do not talk to strange men on the street and at this time of the evening,' my sister retorted.

'Yes,' I agreed, but more for modesty's sake for I was fascinated by the pale gauntness of his face in which his eyes burnt as if from a tortured soul, directly into mine. 'Sir, I am content with things as they are. I am not an artist of commerce, but do them for a hobby.'

'Perhaps, but what harm is there in my seeing your work?'

'There is harm at this time of evening and on the street,' my sister said, raising her voice shrilly as if she might call for help, though it would harm our reputation and her captain was stern enough when it came to female decorum.

'I cannot talk to you, sir,' I answered, and we rushed down the street and into our house.

That was the first time I met him and his eyes and dark form filled my dreams. My work stopped. I spent hours lying as still and as pensive as one of my figures. Then one evening when mother was preparing dinner with the help of Eliza, and father was working late, I draped a shawl over my shoulders, slipped the latch and, taking care to leave the door ajar, darted out onto the street. I consoled myself that it was only for a breath of fresh air, for the evening was close and I had felt hot and confined indoors. I turned from the street and made my way past the market garden and to the stretch of countryside where on occasion my sister and I strolled. I walked along our path and, as the cool air rose around me, I found him at my side.

'I have been waiting for you,' he murmured in that rich voice of his, mellow with a taste of foreignness.

'Sir, there can be no business between us. I am spoken for,' I said, speaking an untruth.

His eyes bored into mine. My body began to tremble. 'Sir,' I implored breathlessly.

'I am not here to hurt you,' he said, his voice almost a whisper. It might have quelled my fears if it was not for the impelling force of his presence which made me blush. My cheeks were red with rich blood, which I hoped he could not see in the darkness.

'Of course, of course,' he said and he took my arm. We walked along the path.

What we talked about, I cannot remember. It could not have been long for my defences were those of a respectable woman. 'Sir, I must return. My father will be there and dinner will be on the table.'

'Go now, for there will be other nights,' he replied, then escorted me back to the market garden and left me.

I slipped into the house and up to my room. No one had noticed my absence, nor did they my subsequent ones.

One evening, I came to him and we walked into the darkness a little and suddenly his face bent towards mine and his arms came out to embrace me.

'No, no, sir, do not take advantage of me,' I cried breathlessly, sinking down upon my knees.

He stood over me and then pressed himself against me. What did he want? I soon found out and thus began my habit, but that night I was young and overwrought by his presence. As he stood there with my face pressed against him, I bit him and tried to jerk away. His hands, so delicate and white but strong, held my head in place for a long moment until I tasted his blood. It was then that he raised me up and stared into my eyes.

'You have bitten me and there is my blood on my lips. You little fool, it will change your life and I need blood for my blood.'

His face descended to my neck and I bit my lips as I felt his sharp teeth, his fangs, pierce the skin and slip into my vein. I must have swooned, for when I came to I was at the door of my house. I entered quietly and went to my room unseen. There were two small wounds in my neck but only a few drops of blood. I wiped them away and wound a thin ribbon around my neck. I gazed into the mirror. Neither experience had shattered me, though they had effected changes. My eyes appeared a darker blue and were filled with mystery. They set off my complexion which was pale and almost bloodless.

I wish that I could say that now began my nightmare, or that there came a time of remorse at eating forbidden fruit and engaging in unseemly rites. I cannot say that there was even a heightened emotion in this encounter with the dark stranger. I fell into a languorous weakened state so that I had to take to my bed. My eyes were enormous in my whitened face and I could not bear to eat even a morsel of food. I longed only for the night and my tryst. He taught me things I had never contemplated, even in dreams, and developed habits in me which gave me pleasure. He also took my blood, took my blood until I died to live in the night. How or why I came to be on this ship is but part of this continuing story and I am wearied of reflection as I am of this carrion.

I fling the drained carcase from me and, surfeited, exult as I hear the rising of the wind. Another gale is rushing from the south to batter us towards the wretched coastline, short of our goal. That sailor was the very last and now there are only corpses left to man my vessel. Not one rises to hinder me as I make my way on deck. I have been careful, for on the voyage I did not want competition for the dwindling food supply. I take the helm, not to guide the ship to safety, but to feel the strength of the tempest rushing us along. She heels and shudders, then scuds maniacally along in a maelstrom of thunder and lightning. One mast snaps and is followed by another.

I scream like a banshee as the vessel hurtles directly at the land. Before our prow is the white surging line of a reef. Spume flies up to drench me. It is the darkest night, not near the hated dawn, and illumination comes from a huge lightning flash which hits the remaining mast and runs down it, leaving a burnt mark in its wake. There is a groan of wrenching timbers as the ship leaps upon the reef. A huge wave batters her across, lifts her up and flings her broadside upon the beach. Another wave and then another pushes her up until she is high and dry. Then the storm recedes as fast as my mood of elation. The night is still except for the scurrying shapes of clouds across the starlit sky. The dark silence of this virgin land overawes me, but dawn is too close and I must seek shelter. I load two bags with my earth and slide down the canting deck, over the side and onto the sand. Holding a sack in each hand, I walk away from the wreck without a backward glance, hurrying inland as the sky lightens in the east. I need to find shelter.

CHAPTER SIX

Gunatinga (Dungeater) was a middle-aged irritable man with bandy legs and thin hair and beard who had no respect amongst his mob either as a hunter or a lover. His unpopularity had turned his face into a scowl and given him an ambition beyond that of the other men of his tribe. He wanted to excel beyond the realms of the possible, as all that was possible had only made him cantankerous. He passed through the camp chewing the ragged end of his beard, constantly on the verge of losing his temper and issuing a challenge to a duel with anyone who glanced his way. This was only show for his fighting prowess was equal to his other attributes. As the result of a duel, he limped from a spear wound in the thigh which had healed slowly to tighten the tendons. His period of incapacitation had not added to his reputation. Unable to hunt, and without a woman, he had had to keep his miserable life going by eating scraps that were flung at him. It was then that he received the name Gunatinga, which caused him to shun his mob as he shunned the name. But Dungeater was not destined to remain the lowest of the low. Contempt drove him into solitude and this raised his standing slightly, for what was solitude but a man leaving the company of humans to contact the spirits and return with powers gained from them; that is, if he was not taken by them. Gunatinga's status did rise, but not by contacting or entering the spirit world. The spirits too, it seemed, shunned him. Instead, as he walked along the beach one day, he came across a whale which was flinging itself upon the shore. He squatted and waited until it had beached itself, then hurried off in a shambling run towards his tribe. As he ran he began to compose a song:

Noongoka kouala,
Noongoka kouala,
Noongoka tichika,
Galbo tichika.

'All of you gather around and come and eat the whale which I have summoned for you.' He was tempted to add other verses detailing the dreaming of this song, but being a man of abrupt words and as no one before had wanted him to speak, or to sing for that matter, he refrained. The tribe sceptically trailed after him to the beach, ready to berate him if what he sang proved to be untrue; but they also were prepared for the opposite, for his keeping apart from them had placed in their heads the idea of the spirits visiting him and perhaps he indeed had become a *maban* or shaman. And so it happened that they came upon the whale and feasted.

Not many months passed before Dungeater came across another beached whale and later a third. His grateful mob now referred to him as Galbol Wednga, the Singer of Whales. At last he had received some respect and was welcomed at the campfires. If it had not been for his gimpy leg and his perpetual scowl, he might have even received a woman of his own, but past treatment had wounded him to the soul and he still kept himself to himself as a shaman with important powers should.

Galbol Wednga was not entirely a fool and upon the occasions when he had come across the beached whales, he had noticed and filed away the times and the type of weather which might drive one of these sea dwellers ashore. This was usually after one of the great storms from the south had hurled itself at the land, driving the beast along and flinging it onto the beach. Last night there had been such a storm. It had struck the coast with undue ferocity and destroyed the dwellings of his tribe. Now his wet and bedraggled mob were in no mood to go off hunting or gathering in the drenched bush, even though the sky was a liquid blue and the sun was bright and warming. Galbol Wednga read the signs and to him came a strong intuition that this day one of the great cetaceans would be waiting for him. He alerted his mob to this by raising his voice in the song, then strode off as quickly as his gimpy leg would allow him. He was halfway to the beach before the others followed him. They straggled in his wake, the prospect of a whale and much feasting raising their spirits.

Singer of Whales reached the beach and stared along the curved stretch of sand that was bounded in both directions by distant headlands. He looked to the left and then to the right. There, towards the far end of the bay and close to the water's edge, was a dark indistinct object. This must be his whale. He sang his song again, then limped towards it, his right foot dragging and his left foot urgent. The others reached the beach when he was some distance along it. They too saw the dark object and turned in that direction. They hesitated when Galbol Wednga stopped and one of his hands motioned to them not to approach. They watched as he bent and stared at the ground. Was this more of his magic, the people wondered as they waited, or was he just showing off as he was inclined to do?

In truth, Galbol Wednga was doing no such thing. He was staring down at the first sculptured image he had ever seen; he did not know what it was. It was half buried in the sand, the figurehead of the *Kore* which had been wrenched from the ship as she was driven ashore. He stared down at the image, overcame his fears and squatted down to uncover more of it. He identified it as a woman coloured like a *moma*, a spirit all white with red painted lips and nipples. Long flowing yellow hair had been carved about the features and down along the sides of the body. Tentatively he pushed out one finger and touched one of the red daubed nipples. Perhaps it was alive, but his finger felt wood and he was relieved and then gladdened, for he realised that the image had been gifted to him and he knew where it had come from. Far to the south lay the country of the giants and on occasion these giants came to his land. They travelled on huge wooden shields through the air or sea pulled along by magic poles covered with feathers. Not only the giants lived there, but also smaller folk on which the giants preyed. This, he exulted, was an image of one of these folks and of great value. Now he would not only be Singer of Whales but would have a secret name, Keeper of the Spirit Image. This object was magic indeed and must be carefully hidden and taken out only at the most secret and hidden of men's rituals. He stared back at his mob. They were far enough away not to see the image. He gestured to them to keep their distance, then turned his back on them to hide what he was doing. He dug into the sand, extending the hole further until the figure sank back. He quickly covered it. Later he could retrieve the sacred image and store it with his magic things which he kept secreted in a cave not too far away.

Having safely hidden his gift, he got to his feet to find that his mob had crept closer. Without a word or sign, he turned, dragged his foot across the area to hide his digging and limped away. Satisfied with his find he was undismayed when he came closer to the dark object to see that it was unlike any whale he had ever seen. Strange objects lay scattered along the beach or bobbed in the surf, but he ignored these, even though behind him his tribe murmured and hung back. He strode on and entered the uncanny. He saw the remains of the feathered sticks which had pulled the shield along. He stared at the shield itself, shaped like a canoe, but vast and made entirely of pieces of wood that fitted together. His mob were on the verge of fleeing, but he turned and beckoned them forward. He, their shaman, walked, or rather limped, towards the shield. As he had given them whales on occasion, now perhaps he was giving them a marvel, they thought.

'It is from the land of giants, far to the south,' exclaimed Galbol Wednga importantly. 'The little spirit people who share that land stole this from the giants and escaped, but see, the giants caught up to them and killed them all.'

There was a collective gasp from the members of his mob, for indeed the sea and beach were littered with corpses, covered in strange skins to keep away the cold of the south, and they were white because, as everyone knew, the sun went from east to west and never from north to south.

'Moma woru maya maya.' Galbol Wednga suddenly sang the words of a spirit devil song. 'We need to conduct the Moma ceremony here and send these spirits back to where they belong. If we do not, they will become devils and haunt us. There is powerful magic here.' He shuddered and the others did the same. 'But,' he continued, 'I will protect you from it. Now let us prepare for the ceremony. See those feathered poles. They have been shattered in the battle that must have been waged here. We must plant them in the ground and connect them together. There is the string which held them together. That too has been severed, but it can still be used. We must fix them now and then after the sun has set we will begin the ceremony.'

They all agreed, but hesitated to begin the work of setting up the lengths of posts which had been broken from the giant shield. Instead, they clustered together and marvelled at the objects which lay scattered over the beach. They kept well away from these as well as from the corpses of the moma for they knew they were still inhabited by their spirits. These would remain until they performed the ceremony and sent them on their way. Galbol Wednga, a confident master of ceremonies now, decided to assert his position. The posts were still connected to the shield by a mass of twisted rope and cordage and none of the others dared to sever them. He looked around and saw what he knew was an axe. An axe different from his own stone axe, but an axe for all that. It was bright and shiny with a smooth wooden handle which went into the bright stone. He wanted such an axe and he bent over and picked it up. How good it felt in his hand. Another gift. He sang a song to propitiate its spirit owner and felt the edge. Never had he felt such a keen blade. 'Wait,' he told his people. 'I have been told to use this ritual object to cut loose the feather sticks. It will protect us from what power runs down the ropes and cords.'

His mob retreated to a good distance while he advanced to where the masts lay, raised the axe and slashed downwards. He was amazed at how quickly the ropes parted, but had he not the power? With a few strokes the masts were free and ready to be erected. It was soon done and the shaman assumed his control again. 'Now return to the camp and collect together a supply of food for our ceremony. We will eat it at the camp, lest these ones lying here smell our cooking fires and rise to take their share. When the sun is setting we shall all return painted for the *Moma* corroboree. There is enough wood here for our ceremonial fires. Now go.'

The blackfellows quickly left the scene of the shipwreck, for there was a sense of foreboding about the place and worse, they felt eyes on them. Galbol Wednga surveyed his scene of triumph and called out to the spirits: 'My secret name is Moma Koopa, Spirit Master, and I will devise a new ceremony which will make me known through all the surrounding countries.' Thus he spoke, and he did achieve fame, but not that which he desired. We called him Puritta Munda, People Killer, as he brought destruction to the mobs living along the south coast.

Now this man of many names dragged his gimpy leg back along the beach as his mob disappeared from sight. He dug up the figurehead and gazed long at it. He knew that it was indeed an object of power and magic and must be speedily put in his keeping place. Taking the heavy female figure in his arms, he felt the curves of her breasts and hips pressing against him as he walked and his penis become erect. He shifted his grip so that the wood rubbed him pleasurably as he limped from the beach and disappeared between two sand dunes.

The beach and the wreck was deserted. The two shattered masts strung with ropes stood upright beside it. The tide rose and the waves moved in and out, disturbing the flotsam which floated about the hulk. From the distant headland, away from the direction in which the blackfellows had disappeared, there came a flash of light reflecting off something bright.

'If we had a cannon, we could have got the lot of them,' the sergeant remarked as he put down the glass.

'But we haven't, have we?' Captain Torrens said sarcastically.

He stared disapprovingly at the detachment of the Fifth Regiment which, under his command, was supposed to defend the settlement against such savages as those who had looted the wrecked vessel.

'One of those blighters went off by himself. Let's get him and interrogate him,' the sergeant suggested with a leer.

'Yes, and he'll know English, won't he? We haven't got time for such fun and games. Why don't you suggest that at the same time we surround the whole damned mob of them with our puny force,' grated the Captain, who was truly sick and tired of being in command of a small force of soldiers who, freed from army discipline by thousands of miles, were now verging on mutiny. Though, by God, just let them try and he would have them swinging in front of the settlement whether it needed defending or not. At that pleasant thought, his dark eyes, hidden under a scowling brow, dwelt briefly on each man. All were scruffy, all were a disgrace to His Majesty's Army. Their faded red coats were open and hung loose about their wasted bodies. Well, supplies had been short and the wreck would give them a chance to replenish them. 'Such an unkempt lot,' he muttered to himself, twisting up his face even more, for he too did not present a perfect picture and why should he in such a hell hole. He tugged at the leather collar of his jacket, then felt a button dangling by a thread before letting his hand fall. Captain Torrens had things other than how he looked to worry about, especially when his moods veered from an almost uncontrollable savagery to a fearful cowardice.

He stared down at the worry the wreck presented. 'Pick up your muskets, check the priming and follow me,' he ordered, suddenly weary of the whole landscape. Then his expression brightened, for the supplies on the *Kore* awaited to be salvaged, that is if the thieving blacks had not destroyed everything. No, they couldn't have, especially not his own private supplies of food and wine. If they had, he would make every single one of the black wretches pay.

'Enough dallying, forward march,' he commanded, his mood rising to an eagerness to get at the wreck. He swung onto his nag which staggered under his weight then lurched forward as he dug his spurs in. He grinned harshly as he led his band of ruffians around the point and onto the beach. As they marched towards the wreck, they spread out into a skirmish line and, under the sergeant's order, primed their muskets.

Captain Torrens was a veteran of the European wars and had seen and survived death, but when he came across the first bodies, his hardened heart gave way to a fright verging on panic. Now, along with the contempt he felt for this land, came fear of the inhabitants. He tried to dismiss them with a curse, but stared down at what would be his fate if they attacked. The male corpses had been badly mutilated at the groin. His eyes darted from corpse to corpse; most had suffered the same fate of emasculation.

'My God,' he exclaimed, his hand going to the front of his trousers. 'Look what the bastards have done to them.'

'It's evil, sir, evil, but it must have been the women. They did the same to the Frenchies on the peninsula,' the sergeant commented above the muttering of the men who, their training coming to the fore, clustered in a tight circle with the muzzles of their muskets pointing outwards. They were ready to defend their privates, to the death if necessary.

So was Captain Torrens, a great bear of a man with the instincts of an animal which shifted from timidity to aggression without much thought.

He was as ready as his men to defend his privates. The prospect of losing their most precious possession had caused them to revert to military discipline. He grinned as he smelt their fear and took advantage of it to issue orders which he knew would be obeyed.

'Sergeant,' he barked, 'you can see what the brutes will do if they catch us off guard. I want half of the men ready to repel the savages if they dare attack us. The others I want to come with me. We must salvage what supplies we can. Be alert and have your muskets at the ready.'

He examined the two masts embedded in the sand. 'Definitely the savages – here is part of their voodoo. Sergeant, stay with those on guard. You other men, don't enter the vessel. See about collecting those casks and bales floating in the sea and littering the beach. Get them all together for transportation back to the settlement.'

Captain Torrens watched his men run to obey his orders, then he dismounted, letting one of his spurs rake the side of the animal. The nag bucked half-heartedly. The scent of death had aroused the old war horse's spirit. He rolled his eyes, kicked out at the captain, then attempted to bite him. Torrens cuffed him over the muzzle and tied him to one of the masts. Now he unlimbered one of his pistols and, pushing down the fear edging into his mind, he approached the wreck with a calm demeanour betrayed only by a slight trembling of his hand. All seemed quiet and peaceful, but who knew how many dozens of savages were lurking in the sand dunes. Suddenly there arose a gale of laughter from off the beach. The rising crescendo broke off as one of the nervous guards fired his musket.

'Oh Christ, it's only one of those laughing jackasses,' Torrens shouted to cover his own nervousness. 'Sergeant, take that man's name. I haven't enjoyed a public flogging for the last week.'

The men turned to him as a body. He stared each one of them down. He had the upper hand and they knew it. Not only was he the commander with special rations which kept him reasonably well fed, but he had other resources as well. And with his bulk he could take on any five of them, and had proved it when they had attempted mass desertion at the arrival of the last supply ship. Still, they remained mutinous, though he had flogged them into a grudging submission. Now, with this massacre by the savages, things had changed and in his favour. 'Men,' he shouted, 'stay at your posts. These savages are all around us.'

The soldiers started and turned to the hinterland. As one man, their muskets rose. 'No, no,' he shouted. 'Don't waste your powder. We might need it before this day is done.' And leaving them with that thought, he grimaced with satisfaction and went to the wreck.

He laughed as he clambered onto the canting deck. He made his way to a hatchway, pushed his way through and came across more mutilated corpses. It made him snarl, for it meant that the savages had penetrated into the wreck and got at the supplies. Well, they would be taught a lesson. When his change next came upon him, he would savage them with a savagery which would go beyond their own. His face turned vicious then just as suddenly went blank as he strove to push down such thoughts, for such proclivities – which others labelled cruelty – had wrecked his promising career and exiled him to the ends of the earth. Still, he could not suppress the wild urges sweeping up to replace any other emotions as he contemplated a scene of decay and butchery that would have driven other men into terror. He was in the forecastle now and it was splattered with blood and corpses. He stared at the naked and torn bodies and licked his lips as his mind filled with dark thoughts centred on blood-letting. There were more bodies below decks, but thankfully he came upon a cask of harsh rum which he broached and upended over his gulping mouth. Damn, it felt good and helped him to avoid any desire of fingering the wounds of the beckoning corpses. Sated, he flung the cask away from him and watched it smash against a bulkhead. If the others came aboard and found it open they would empty it, and he could not afford to have the soldiers drunk when the natives might return at any time. Well, let them return, let them, for they had to pay for what they had done here. In fact, he decided as the rum rose to his head, this very day they would pay. He would give them a taste of their own bloody medicine which would put a stop to their pilferage. Captain Torrens's exultation rose even higher when he found his own supplies untouched. Unwilling to let others onto the wreck, he lugged the six chests onto the deck, then ordered a soldier to come and stack them on the beach. That done, he licked his lips and turned to shout at the sergeant. 'Summon the men and find them something to eat from what's on the beach. We march in an hour after those natives. The perpetrators of this atrocity must be punished and I swear by God that before this day is through, they will be.'

CHAPTER SEVEN

This is a cruel land and I welcomed its sense of cruelty when it came to me far out on the ocean. I knew that I was more than a match for it and could meet savagery with savagery; but still this earth, this ground, is alien to me. It is not my earth and the ground here cannot be my resting place. I need my rich loam to survive and have spread it over the cool dampness of the floor at the inner reaches of the cave where no light can possibly reach me. Light. I cannot abide that harsh light of day. I need the sweet darkness with the soft gleam of the moon and stars bathing my body with their gentle healing powers. Now, safely on my earth and away from that accursed light, I recline and wait for that sweet feeling of lassitude which overcomes me as the sun reaches the zenith of his climb. I wait on, but although the weakness comes it does not bring surcease and I lie here awake, letting my mind wander back to the *Kore* and how I milked the cattle penned thereon. I smell again the blood flowing and now feel my hunger stirring within me like some stretching beast. Gradually my mind frees itself of memory and drifts further out onto the ocean where it encounters a vessel labouring under torn sails towards the land. The boy dog holds the helm and his mind opens to allow me to enter effortlessly. I direct his hands to turn the wheel slightly, correcting the course so that the schooner, for such she is, will sail directly to where the wreck of the *Kore* rests. I am about to move further into his mind, then I become aware that there are others who are sensitive to my presence. One of them reaches out to make contact and sings a song which drives me back to my cave.

The floor is too hard and my layer of earth too thin. I cannot sleep and need my own earth, thick and loamy and extending down to the earth's core. How I long for the comfort of my box. How I wish that I had taken it up and carried it here, for I have strength beyond that indicated by my slight physique, but the dawn was nigh then and I had to hurry to seek shelter. I lie back pensively and thoughts of home and my master sweep me away into a mood of bittersweet nostalgia, when the blood was tart on my lips and the countryside was soft and quiet under the shedding moon or the downpours of autumn. But in winter the snow lay thick upon the ground and hunting was often unprofitable. It was the lack of prey that drove me into the cities and the gay life of the evening in which I hunted among the low and unseemly. It was then that I met the Captain, my sister's husband, on the prowl for young flesh rather than blood. By then I had changed so much, was so avid and eager, that it was of no great matter to enter into his company and even onto his ship where I found that he had a liking for sodomy. No great matter, for I was beyond such trifling morality as long as I could keep the other safe. I had grown weary of the night life and of the city with its smoke and thin blood. It was he whom I persuaded to secret me aboard his ship, the *Kore*. It was he who carried my box on board and stowed it safely. And it was he who was the first to go, though I rationed out my food supply as the vessel ploughed through the seas, month after month, until corpses littered the vessel and the prey turned wary. I trapped the last one and bled him dry as the coastline came into view and, and ...

A sound from just outside my refuge rouses me from my lethargy. I recall seeing some rude native artefacts to the left side of the cave mouth as I entered. Beyond noting them, I had paid them no heed, for what interest could they hold for me? Now there comes a scuffling and a dragging. I may not be able to bear the light, and even though in the day I am weak, I can still bring whoever it is that disturbs me to where I am lying. I reach out and he does not have the mind to overcome me, though his terror of the dark interior of this cavern makes him hesitate within the light at the entrance.

'Come to me,' I gently urge him. 'Come to me, though I cannot call you sweet. Come to me, my uncouth one.' I ease him gently into the cave and the darkness beyond. I see that he is carrying the figurehead from the vessel and that the smooth curved wood has aroused him. 'Come to me,' I call again. 'Come to me, set down that graven image and you shall meet the Kore herself. Come and feel her livid flesh instead of dead wood. Ah, you have found me.'

I sit up and wrap my arms around his waist. He is petrified with terror and as stiff as the figurehead he held. I soothe him as I would a doll, stroking him, and discover that he is somewhat different from other men, that is those of England. There is a long slit where there should be none. As I run my tongue along it, it reminds me of my own, though he is male enough. I take him into my mouth and give him such pleasure that his fright recedes as he groans in ecstasy. The tip of my tongue travels along inside him until it reaches the end of the slit where it delicately explores a scar. It is some savage mutilation, but I am glad of it. I break the skin and let the blood trickle down my throat. Just a little bite that pierces the old scar tissue but does not go deep to the vein, for I have need of this rude person. In this vast and cruel land I am entirely alone and must have someone to do my bidding, especially when I am incapacitated by the day. In his mind I explain to him his new position as I give him an advancement on his first wage.

'Now I am sucking on you and my tongue is in you. Now I am tasting your blood and I shall be your mistress. What is your language to me? I brush it aside and talk to you in pictures in your head. Yes, you understand, don't you! Now, what will I call you? Yes, Renfield. Can you pronounce that in your rude language? "Renfiel". Then so be it, that is your name and when we are apart, I shall call you and you will come to me.'

I have a last taste of his blood, then the other as he spends himself. His taste is different from what I have been accustomed to. When it is over, I rise up from my knees and jab my nail into my arm to bring blood. I pull his head down and put his lips on my wound, holding him tightly so that he must fill his mouth with my blood then swallow it. He does so and I have a servant.

'Suck again my servant,' I command and he does so. He is mine and shall remain so until I no longer need him. Until then, if needs be, I shall use him as a milch cow to satisfy my thirst. I order him to sit and wait out the day. I examine his mind and see that the moon is waxing and that the tempest has passed. 'Good. Sit by me and be quiet,' I order as he begins to speak. 'Sleep until the darkness arrives,' I command him. Thinking of the pleasure he has had, he falls asleep to dream of it while I remain awake and feel the hunger growing. But I will not take more from him as yet.

The soldier lifted his pannikin, drained it and stared into the fire with haunted eyes. 'Christ, only five of us and after what we did to the savages they'll be down on us for sure. That Cap'n ... well it might have been proper to hang the blighters, but did he have to slash open their bellies? You can smell the stench almost from here. And there's only us five here.' He refilled his pannikin.

'They had to be taught a lesson,' the sergeant replied wearily. He too had not liked the executions, no matter how justified. He dove his own mug into the broached cask of rum and drank deeply. 'He'll be back tomorrow with the carts for the supplies and we had to protect them, though after what we did there won't be a savage within miles. They've been taught a lesson good and proper and so there's enough of us to help ourselves to what we need. Drink up, for we'll not get much of this when he's around.'

'Aye, he's a right savage, but then so are they. Still, he could have left more of the men here with us.'

'Naw, he needed them to carry away his own grub and grog,' another soldier put in. 'He's a brute and always out for himself.'

The sergeant protested at the attack. 'Well, he got the thing done, didn't he? I expect you lot would still be digging now to bury those bodies if he hadn't got them natives doing it. And you know what they did to them, so fair's fair.'

'Aye, first you get them to bury our dead, then you make them dead. But who's going to bury them? I won't.'

'Let them hang, I say, let them hang and rot. Drive the lesson home to them, that's what I say. Treat them with kindness and there'll be a spear in your throat before you know it.'

The soldier's words were his last, for a spear whizzed from the shadowy darkness and pierced his throat with such force that the barb was forced through. His comrades stared in drunken stupefaction for a long moment, then grabbed for their muskets and fired into the surrounding sand dunes. They quickly reloaded then waited for an attack. Instead, from the far side of a sand dune there came a woman's plaintive wail. 'Help me, please help me.'

Sergeant: 'There's a woman out there, a white woman. She must be from the ship. We've got to save her.'

Soldier: 'How can we? We bloody well can't save ourselves!'

The four stared down at the man writhing on the ground. A gurgling sound came from his throat and where the long spear stuck up, blood spurted forth to soak into the sand.

Sergeant: 'If we stand like this with the fire behind us, we'll end up like him. Get on your bellies, you lot.'

Second soldier: 'What will we do? They're all around us, I know they are. They're so black they merge with the shadows.'

He raised his musket and fired. They heard the ball strike the side of the sand dune. The woman's voice called out urgently, 'Oh, please help me. Oh please'.

Soldier: 'Oh damn it, help yourself!'

Sergeant: 'No firing, less I give the word. You might hit her, poor thing.'

Woman: 'Help me. The savage was hit, he has run away. Help me before he returns with more of them.'

Second soldier: 'It's a bloody old trick, Sarge. Best we stay put.'

Sergeant: 'Aye, and when did these bloody savages speak English? Look, the moon is coming up and that'll give us light enough. She's a white woman. God knows what she suffered when the ship drove ashore and those savages began their work. We've got to go to her. We're coming, madam, or girl, keep calling. We're on our way. Keep calling to guide us to you.'

Woman: 'Hurry sir, hurry, I am so afraid. This way, this way. Hurry and succour me before he returns and inflicts himself on me again.'

Sergeant: 'Keep calling, keep calling, we'll be with you this instant.'

The men warily left the fire and advanced into the shadows of the dune. Suddenly there was a single shot, then screams which tapered off into the sounds of slurping. Renfiel limped out of the darkness and stared down with malicious glee at the expiring soldier before leaning on the spear and driving it further into the sand. Not satisfied with this, he twisted it from side to side causing the man to gurgle horribly. Then, leaving the pinned man to die, he picked up a red coat and tried it on. Amelia came from the darkness, her mouth red and dripping with blood, and examined the soldier as he gave a shudder and expired. 'Such a waste, such a waste of living blood,' she exclaimed, bending down and poking at the wound with her finger. She lifted it to her lips and licked at the blood. 'Too much rum as always,' she said, making a face.

Amelia stared intently at Renfiel who cowered as she spoke within his mind. 'Come, there is work to be done. I must have my box and it must be in the cave by dawn. And when this is done I have another task for you. Find out where these men come from, then return to me in the evening. It is a simple enough thing to do, especially when you wear one of their red coats. You look half civilised already and what is more you have become a killer of men today, that is if you have not already killed many men in your rude state which lacks sanctions against taking human life. If you serve me well, perhaps one day I will allow you to sup on their blood as I do. It lacks, I assure you, the savour of yours. Now come here, the hunt has made me excited and I want to sip on you before your work commences. You have a wild taste which is so delicious in comparison to that of these rum-sodden curs. Leave that cask alone. You may eat, but do not drink, for that poison will contaminate your blood.'

CHAPTER EIGHT

The sudden squall which hit us almost put an end to our voyage. What saved us was the short endurance of the tempest: it rolled over us, stripped off our sails, then rushed off towards the mainland leaving us wallowing behind in a heavy swell. The squall struck in the darkest portion of the night without warning. One moment I was dozing over the listless wheel, then the next I was fighting to keep her headed into the waves. Without sails it was hopeless and so I let her ride along with the waves towards the land marked in the distance by the boom of thunder and the flash of lightning. Wadawaka had rushed on deck to stand at my side, but there was little he could do to right the situation.

'We have no sails,' he commented dryly, 'and must find some. The only thing we can do is to rig up a jib that will bring us to the land if this breeze keeps up. It will give us more steerage at least.'

He roused the rest of the men, whom he had trained into a tolerable crew, then had the women stitch together a jib sail from the remnants he had ordered cut down from our masts. By dawn everything was as shipshape as could be under the circumstances and we made our way slowly towards the coastline under our single sail. Wadawaka took the helm and I went into the cabin to enjoy a well-earned sleep. Well-earned but not enjoyable, for the dreams which had plagued me since my transformation came to me again. This time I saw a vessel strike the shore and worse, far worse than the great rendering crash which sent the masts over the side, was the fact that all of the crew were corpses. A single person alone survived: a female ghost who left the stricken vessel lugging two sacks. She made her way inland where she took refuge in the recesses of a dismal cavern. Thankfully at that point the dream ended and I managed to wake somewhat refreshed to partake of our rations which was salt junk made into some sort of hash and flat cakes of bread. After this, night descended on us again and Jangamuttuk began cracking his clapsticks and singing doleful verses from the Ghost Dreaming.

At last he stopped to exclaim, 'They are near. I feel them close. This will keep them at bay,' and he began singing again.

Wadawaka explained to me that this was indeed true. 'Yes,' he said, 'they have a settlement to the east of us, but it should be all right if we keep alert and hurry our departure. If we could sail on, I would, but the damage must be repaired. Let us hope that the wreck is deserted and we can go in, get what we want and be away without trouble.'

'What wreck?' I asked with a quaver in my voice.

'The one we must make for,' he replied, 'or else this voyage is at an end. Without sails it is impossible for us to continue.'

I nodded dismally, looking up at our bare masts and the billowing jib which was taking us at a slow pace to the mainland. I felt apprehension creep into my mind, for that dream and the place where the wreck lay was clear in my mind. I looked beyond the masts, up into the sky where the moon was gorging herself on the stars, becoming fatter and fatter from her constant feeding. How bright her face was and how calm the sea. Small white ponies galloped beside us and our prow broke the water without a murmur. Somehow I missed the shook-shook of our sails as they strained under a steady wind, then the image of the grey shrouds of bat wings came to me and I felt a calling which I must answer.

I took over the helm and kept the vessel steady before the breeze which continued to push us towards our destination, or rather just west of our destination. I carefully made the course correction; now we were aimed straight at the position where the wreck lay beached upon the land. If the breeze continued behind us, we should reach there by mid afternoon.

Wadawaka lowered the jib and then dropped a sea anchor which somewhat impeded our passage through the water. He raised a telescope to his eye and carefully studied the nearby coast, moving it slowly along a line of shattering waves which indicated a reef.

'There is,' he said, lowering the glass and passing it to me, 'a narrow passage through the reef and into the calmer waters beyond. It is both good and bad, for we shall be sheltered from the open sea but first we must get through without striking or holing our hull.'

He handed me the telescope and I aimed it along his pointing finger. There was a break in the swirling white waters and the waves swept through and on to dissipate in the calmness.

'How shall we manage?' I queried.

'By faith, good fortune and excellent seamanship,' he replied, then ordered the jib set. The breeze dragged us along slowly for he still kept the sea anchor out.

'Now, you take the helm and keep her steady on that spot where there is a swirl of water,' he ordered me. 'I will take soundings as we proceed, for all the good that will do if our luck runs out.'

As we neared the froth of water, the wheel became restless in my hands. I held her steady, as steady as I could, as Wadawaka called out the soundings. The depth was more than enough and this meant that the reef fell away sharply on the ocean side. Our schooner inched her way towards the entrance of the narrow passageway. Suddenly there was a crash and our vessel was flung to the larboard edge of the reef as the current rushing through the gap caught us. A long rasping came and with it rose the voice of Jangamuttuk singing us to safety. We swept through into the calmer waters beyond.

'Down the jib,' Wadawaka shouted and rushed to lower the sail himself. Our sea anchor now held us away from the beach and we could see the wreck clearly.

Wadawaka raised the telescope again and carefully examined it. 'A brigantine from the looks of her and she must have been carrying supplies. Now let me see ...' and he swept his glass over the vessel. 'We are in luck for she is deserted. Now the beach ...' He swept the shoreline. 'No movement, unless they are hidden behind the vessel, for she lies side on to the shore. But we must go in. If only we had a whaleboat we might quickly transfer what we need from a distance, but our dinghy is too small for the job. Well, it is to be the jib again. Keep the helm steady and I will take soundings again. If it is possible I want to bring her right alongside the wreck as the tide is on the rise. You men, be ready with the anchor. I don't want to run her aground.'

Slowly, under Wadawaka's direction, we inched towards the wreck which, in her position, might render us a safe mooring as if at a regular quay. The water rapidly shallowed, but not enough for us to strike bottom.

'Now swing the helm hard over,' Wadawaka shouted to me. I did so, bringing her broadside to the waves which pushed us with only a little force against the brigantine. Enough ropes hung from her sides for our crew to quickly secure our vessel. This done, we took stock of our situation.

'Someone has been here before us,' our captain remarked. 'Let us hope that they have left enough for our needs.'

He lightly sprang up on the side of the wreck which was canted over towards the land and disappeared over the top. Anxiously we waited for him to reappear. It was some time before he did so and while we waited we became aware of the foreboding atmosphere that hung over the wreck. Our nostrils quivered with a stink of decaying flesh, human flesh. My dream knowledge told me that it came from the ghosts that had crewed the vessel. At last, to our relief, Wadawaka appeared and slid down to us.

'There are enough sails in the sail locker for us to adapt to our needs, and also provisions with which we can stock our schooner, but ...' He hesitated, looked grave, then apprehensive. 'We must move quickly for this is an ill-omened place for us to tarry in. Jangamuttuk, come with me. I have need of your shaman skills to allay any bad spirits which might seek to do us harm.'

He and Jangamuttuk clambered onto the side of the wreck and disappeared over the top. There was a sudden cry from my father, followed by the sound of his clapsticks as he took up the ghost refrain.

They made of me a ghost down under,
Made of me a place to plunder,
They made of me a ghost down under,
Please have pity on these ghosts now under.

Curiosity made us wait no longer. All of us, men and women, scrambled up the side of the wreck and then hesitated as we reached the top. There was a short drop to the deck which canted down to where the far side rested almost on the beach. But it was not this that stopped us; it was the sight that paralysed us with fear, a fear which had caused our flight and which now had preceded us to this shore. There on the sand sat my father, Jangamuttuk, beating his clapsticks and intoning his doleful song. There sat Wadawaka beside him and there in front of them ten dead black bodies hung swaying in the breeze. These were covered over with buzzing flies. It had been their rotting bodies that we had smelt. Now the women gave a heart-rending cry and slid down the deck and onto the sand where they commenced their wailing, beating their breasts and foreheads in sadness for these men who had been slain in their prime.

We men followed and took up Jangamuttuk's doleful chant: 'They made of me a ghost down under, Made for me a place to plunder, way down under.'

I felt my eyes fill with tears and I could not at first bear to look at the hanging dead bodies. At last I found the strength to glance, then stared as if I could not drag my eyes away from them. The shattered tops of the masts of the brigantine had been buried in the sand and then a spar had been lashed between them, tied securely so that it would remain firm under the weight and thrashings of ten human beings. Then, in order for the murderers to do their work without overly stretching, a long narrow trench had been dug underneath. Nooses had been tied at intervals along the spar and through these the heads of the unfortunate victims had been thrust. Then, from the marks along the edge of the trench, their feet had been kicked away from under them and they had swung out into space, choking at the end of the ropes. Some of them, I saw, had tried to swing back to the side of the trench and thus lessen the terrible agony, but their feet had been kicked away by heavy ghost boots. I stared at the twisted faces with the swollen tongues alive with flies. They protruded like diseased slugs from mouths wide open, gasping for air, wide open to force through a final breath which was blocked by the constricting rope. I stared. I could smell the blood congealed in dead veins. I inhaled a stronger stench and glanced down from the faces to a further horror: each corpse had been slashed across the stomach, had been hacked open by a blunt instrument, for the wounds were not clean cuts and seemingly had been prolonged to add to the agony of the suffocating victims. I saw how the blood had flown out along with the intestines which bulged and oozed harsh fluids and odours. It was too much for me to bear and I retreated to the wreck. I vomited and slumped down in the space between side and deck. It was there that Wadawaka found me.

'A bad business lad, a bad business,' he said, laying a consoling hand on my shoulder. 'Best we get away from this place as quickly as we can. You and I must leave the others to their mourning and set our schooner to rights.'

I thrust aside my trepidation and took refuge in work. Others soon joined us, for all wanted to get away from that evil place. Sails began to be cut and stitched to fit our masts, kegs and barrels were investigated for what would serve us on our voyage, and what we could use we began taking aboard. It was while we were engaged in our tasks that my father came to Wadawaka and said, 'I have flown away from this sorry sight and scouted out the land to the east. There stands the ghost settlement. They are responsible for this. What can we do to revenge these poor blackfellows?'

Wadawaka, always the practical man, replied, 'Best that we leave this awful place with the next ebb tide which is still some hours off. This will give you time, if needs be, to bury these poor fellows properly and sing their spirits to rest. It is all that we can do, for who knows what other baleful forces lurk here. Best that we leave and do what necessary repairs on the open sea.'

We were all depressed and there was no disagreement. Massacres such as this were what we were fleeing from after trying and failing to prevent them on our island. It was best that we put the dreary scene behind us and sail on towards our hoped-for refuge, for if we tarried we too might end up as these poor blackfellows. Holding such thoughts and feelings, we forced ourselves to return to the beach and the terrible sight. Jangamuttuk, Master of the Ghost Dreaming, was beginning to give his instructions for a funeral service for the murdered blackfellows when from the sand dunes at the back of the beach a spear whanged out and struck beside him. We leapt to our feet, not to defend ourselves, but to take shelter behind a stack of kegs which had been piled on the sand as if for transportation elsewhere. More spears flashed towards us. Some were so badly aimed that they struck the hanging bodies. Swarms of black flies rose in the air. Then came shouts and threats. A mob of angry and wailing blackfellows burst from between two dunes and rushed down towards us. They surrounded us. We were at their mercy. Would they show any when they themselves had received none?

CHAPTER NINE

It seemed to be the end of all our hopes and dreams. Behind us, indeed, was the wreck and beyond that the schooner to which we might have retreated except for the probability of any number of spears striking us down as we scrambled up the steeply canting deck. Such a retreat was too perilous to attempt so, as always in such moments of danger, we looked towards our shaman who held up in front of him the message stick of Waai as a talisman. But the sight of the bodies of their fellow tribesmen swinging in the breeze and the rank odour of their ruptured bellies enraged the blackfellows to a frenzy. The foremost of them bent his arm then straightened it. A spear flew directly at Jangamuttuk and would have struck the message stick and his torso if he had not, with a skill learnt in many an encounter, swayed to one side, letting the weapon whiz harmlessly past.

Their faces were bloated with rage and their bodies quivered with the urge for vengeance. Their arms drew back, but just when all seemed lost a figure limped onto the beach and with a high-pitched 'cooee' made them hesitate. The newcomer was clad in a ghost soldier's red jacket beneath which his pearl shell pubic covering dangled between two bare legs, ill-matching both coat and each other. They looked like two bent and twisted sticks. On these he sought to strut forward importantly, though one did not work as the other so that he rolled towards us with a gait which we would have found ludicrous if we were not on the verge of being slaughtered.

'I am no longer Galbol Wednga,' this person now exclaimed in a reedy voice, striving for authority. 'I am Spirit Master and some of those who came from the land of the giants in that vast shield and murdered our tribesmen are no more. This covering I wear is from one of them. It has power and all spirits will flee in dismay when they see it.'

He reached the bodies hanging from the spar and declaimed, 'How sad, how sad. If I had been here, they would be still alive.' Then he turned on us. 'Who are these strangers? They are not spirits, for their skins are as black as ours and everyone knows that in the land far to the south the clouds are impenetrable and the skins of those who live there are white. Who are they?' he demanded again.

There was a muttering from his fellows for they had been too enraged for thought. Now they lowered their weapons, though they kept alert. Jangamuttuk took this opportunity to come forward. He walked boldly into stabbing range of their spears and held out the message stick. The person, Spirit Master, came and took it.

'Arrh, it is from a fellow shaman of a tribe now separated from us by the settlement which has been constructed by those spirits who seek to slaughter all of us. I know him. Waai, a Crowman. He must be warned of this evil upon our land. We must remove the strangers ...' Instantly spears were raised and arms drew back to cast them. 'No, no,' Spirit Master spluttered hurriedly. 'Not these strangers, whoever they are, but those white *moma* who have settled between Crow's land and mine. Who are you, mob, anyway?' he demanded of us. 'What are you doing on our shores?'

The tension lessened enough for me to smile in anticipation. I half expected my father to go into an elaborate pantomime like that which had elicited such mirth from Crow and his people, but this was not to be as we had perfectly understood Spirit Master's words. Now my father began: 'I am Master of the Ghost Dreaming and we have come from a land which has been overrun by the *moma*. We called them *nam*, but it seems that both *nam* and *moma* are the same. They come from a cold land, though they said it lies to the east rather than to the south. We are fleeing from them...'

Spirit Master broke in rudely, 'They are from the south, from the land of giants. I have seen it in my spirit vision, thus it is not to be doubted.'

'That may be so, and giants were indeed mentioned. They even have a story called Jack and the Beanstalk. Yes, you are correct, for after all my own powers are slight ...' and so Jangamuttuk sought to pacify the person who claimed to be a shaman, and succeeded for he positively beamed under the flattery.

'Yes, yes, times are awry,' he declaimed. 'It is for powerful men such as myself to set them straight. I will send a message to Crow and ask for his help in ridding us of these spirits, ghosts, demons, or what you will. If you had had me on your island, you would not have had to flee,' he boasted, then turned to his mob and ordered them to take down the bodies. 'We must perform our funeral service and send the souls who are trapped in these decaying bodies on their way. As it is our ceremony and for our kinsmen, these strangers are forbidden to attend. Let them camp there!' His hand spun around from sea to land and finally settled on the space between the sand dunes from which he had emerged. 'I have,' he boasted, 'slaughtered the spirits there and thus made it again safe for humans.'

'Kin must bury their kin, certainly,' agreed Jangamuttuk, 'but when the sad duty of sending them off is done, all of us might perform the special ceremony which will help us psychically in our fight against the *moma.* Crow has passed on to me this ceremony and I know all of the songs and rituals.'

'Yes, yes,' spluttered Spirit Master, 'but it shall not be done by you. Crow will come and give me the ceremony to perform. It is mine by right of my skill. It should belong to me, for I am Spirit Master ...'

'One shaman is powerful, two are more so, and three will relieve us of all danger,' Jangamuttuk broke in softly.

'True, true, especially when one is the most powerful of all. And I will need attendants. Now I must send these poor fellows on their way.'

His mob had taken down the bodies of their kinsmen and now, with much calling on the souls to follow their earthly remains, they left, leaving us alone on the beach.

It was still light and we had much to do. We spread the sails out upon smooth sand and Wadawaka measured them to length and breadth. He cut them and the women began stitching the edges and corners so that the tackle could be attached. Under the direction of Fada's wife they had learnt how to sew and this was a good skill which was ever in use, unlike that which he had taught to the men, another kind of sewing – of seeds, which was useless to us as yet. While the women sewed the men hastened to load the provisions and other things Wadawaka selected from the wreck. Our schooner was small in comparison to the brigantine and we could carry only what was absolutely needed. By the time the sun was writhing towards his nest under the horizon, we had stowed everything away and the only task that remained was to repair the rigging which we would do the following morning.

'Now let us go to our camping place as designated by that Spirit Master,' Jangamuttuk said, 'though whether he is indeed a master or not is another thing. A shaman has skills but hides them from the ears and eyes of others. He is too ready to talk of his exploits, but never mind, he did save us and so we must follow, to a certain extent, what he has suggested.'

With some provisions gleaned from the *Kore* – for such was the name I read from the stern of the wreck using the skill of deciphering letters which Fada had imparted to me – we went behind the dune and came across evidence that the ghosts had been there. An empty keg lay on its side beside the remains of a fire, and worse, far worse, we glanced up and saw that we had stumbled into an ambush. On the top of the next sand dune, edged by the light, sat five soldiers with their weapons pointing down at us. We backed away slowly, but then Jangamuttuk gave a laugh and with a courage which bordered on foolhardiness scrambled up the side of the dune to where the soldiers waited.

'Dead as the poor blackfellows on the beach,' he called down to us.

Only Wadawaka and myself had the nerve to climb up to him. It was as he had said. The five soldiers, one without his red coat, were dead. Lengths of broken spar had been fastened to their hands and they had been bound in a sitting position to other pieces which had been jammed vertically into the ground.

'Well, at least Spirit Master might have had a hand in getting rid of these ghosts,' my father declared, pointing at the throat of one of the soldiers. An ugly wound showed where a spear had gone in and been pulled out.

We came down from the dune and left the hollow, deciding to find another spot which was not under the surveillance of the dead. As we set up camp some distance away, Jangamuttuk talked over the matter. He decided that the killings could not have been the work of a single person such as Spirit Master, though one of the soldiers indeed had been speared by a blackfellow.

Wadawaka thought it over and replied, 'It is easy to read the signs and add to them the fact that the *Kore* has also been revisited after the murders of the blackfellows. They came by sea and by land. I saw the ruts of carts in the sand and the ropes hanging from the side had been used to tie up a boat. Also much of the cargo had been disturbed and things taken away. The ghosts located the wreck, hung those poor blackfellows, then left a guard behind. Those soldiers over there. They were killed by someone else as well as that crippled one, for I doubt that he could have killed all five of them, even from ambush. When the other ghosts returned, they arranged those corpses as a warning to the local mob who they thought had taken revenge for the earlier slayings.'

'You have read it right,' Jangamuttuk agreed. 'I was waiting for the lad to deduce what happened, but his eyes are as dim as his brain. It seems that not only are there ghosts, but spirits as that person has told us, and that ghosts and spirits and humans do not get on very well together. We should help the locals in getting rid of them.'

'It would be best that we leave at once, but the sails and rigging must be set to rights first,' Wadawaka replied. 'We might help, and even if we don't we still have to be on guard. We should search the wreck for weapons just in case whatever killed the ghosts returns, or for that matter if they themselves return for more of the cargo.'

'None of those boom-boom weapons,' Jangamuttuk protested. 'Let me construct psychic defences against any visitation. I will weave spirit catchers to entangle them be they spirits or ghosts.'

'But the ghosts are as humans,' replied Wadawaka, 'and if they return they will return in force.'

'Well, what matter. We will have our spears at hand, but best that we avoid those muskets. The noise might bring others down upon us. We also have those knives and hatchets from the wreck which will be of more use than spears or guns. At night a spear flies wide of its mark, but a knife or axe will always find its target when it is held in the hand.'

And so it was decided, though I kept my pistol close to me which would serve me in close encounters if any eventuated. After we had eaten and the moon rose bloated from her feasting on the stars, there came to me an urge to roam the hinterland. I had come to accept my ability to transform and knew that I had some control over my Dreaming animal form. I decided to relieve myself away from the camp. The cool light of the moon flowed over me as my urine whistled down. I shook out the last few drops, assumed my Dreaming shape and trotted off into the bush.

I was loath to take to the air. I felt so ungainly there, often unable to control my direction owing to my lack of experience. The sky for me was for flight and refuge. If I was badly frightened I could take to the air where few enemies might follow, but for the plenitude of smells and sounds in which I luxuriated, I needed the bush with its welcoming shadows and prey. I snuffled up the scent of one such. A bandicoot! How long was it since I had tasted one of those small tender and juicy creatures? I imagined crunching the bones between my strong teeth and saliva dripped from my jaws as my nostrils quivered from its scent. My ears tracked its slight rustles as it moved away from me unhurriedly, for the breeze had turned to come from inland, warm and smelling of dust without a trace of moisture within the particles. The bandicoot could not detect my scent but he had sharp ears and if I betrayed myself by a sound the ratlike creature would break into a darting scuttle which would take it beyond my slavering jaws.

My body sank close to the ground and I crept forward, careful not to place a paw upon the ground unless it was free of twigs which might snap and betray my presence. I made my way silently after him as he entered a clump of trees surrounding a pool of water. The moon was swollen and beamed down. Would the animal cast a glance over its shoulder and make out my slinking form before I gained the shelter of the trees? No. He continued on unhurriedly. By the time I passed into the shadows of the first tree I was very close behind him. I drew nearer, anxious, but not too anxious, to have him in my jaws. Then, as I judged that I was close enough for a sudden dash, my paw came down upon a twig. There was a harsh snap and instantly I leapt forward and my jaws closed over the warm furry body. The bandicoot writhed and tried to break free. I clamped my jaws firmly then, as he stopped his struggles for a moment, I unclamped them and fastened onto his hind-quarters. I tasted blood, eucalyptus sweet and acrid, as my teeth came together. The bandicoot went into a frenzy, but I lifted him up and shook him until he was still. Now I held the carcase between my front paws and using my incisor teeth carefully peeled the skin away. I ripped at the naked flesh, then plunged my muzzle into the body, filling my nostrils with its rich bloody tang. Aroused by the odour, I tore at the carcase, crunching bones and flesh together as I fed.

My feeding over, I licked my lips and padded further into the clump of trees. The bandicoot had satisfied my hunger and lust for the kill. I trotted without due care to the billabong at which I slaked my thirst. I licked a few drops of water from my jaws, then padded off along the dried-up river bed, exulting in the night life all around me.

Then, into my mind there came a calling. Puzzled, I hesitated and sniffed the breeze. I could smell no one, especially a human, then the call came again and from an easterly direction. Without thought, I turned and trotted off towards it. During my stalking I had wandered a few miles inland and now I was moving towards the sea, but at a diagonal to the camp. I was going due east, parallel to the coast, towards where the coastal plain met the inland plateau in a series of rough stone ledges. They hurt the soft underpadding of my paws. I picked my way carefully, became a human thinking within a dog's body and as I lingered on a thought, my four feet broke their rhythm which kept them apart and I fell entangled in a heap. I snarled and went on. Ahead of me I saw the dark entrance to a cave. I tried to change back, but found that I could not. I eyed the opening into the earth and hesitated, but dingoes are curious animals and so I trotted forward. Dingoes are also wary animals, so my trot became a walk. I crept on and there came to me the stink of decaying flesh. The thought of a feast of rotting meat urged me forward. I was almost at the cave entrance when a human voice sounded. I stopped and my hackles rose.

'Here, boy, here,' a female voice called softly.

In spite of myself, I felt my tail wagging. The female called again and I gleefully trotted to where she stood with a hand outstretched. She was just about to pat me when there was a flash of red light from the sky. The woman stepped back into the cave entrance with a cry, her right hand clutching her left arm.

My human mind asserted itself but I did not flee. I glanced up into the sky and saw a huge thing flap across the face of the moon. Some person rode upon its back. A familiar scent came to me as the thing swooped low and then my mother stood before me.

'Get back to the camp now, boy. Go on, scat,' she ordered. I turned and trotted off, then stopped a few yards away looking back over my hindquarters. 'Go on, get!' she shouted again. 'I'll handle this thing here.'

My life in this desolate region is becoming more ordered. I have a servant who will see to my needs when the sun governs the sky. I even have the chance of adding another person to my retinue, for the one which bit me is at the *Kore*. I call to him. He assumes his dog form and trots away from his fellows, but his unformed mind is easily distracted and he does not come directly to me. Still, I enjoy the stalking of his prey, the sharp teeth ripping into the flesh and the tart taste of blood, which on this land has a particular fragrance which increases my thirst rather than allays it, but then I have not drunk myself this night, and when the dog comes I fantasise about what I will do to him, whatever shape he may be in. There he is and he comes as a dog. Now I will take him.

Alas, it is not to be. As I reach down to him, a searing red light flashes down from the sky and strikes me. The pain is such that I almost sink to my knees, but as is the way of our kind I ignore it and step back into the cave entry. I am angered to see my prey lope off and also startled at seeing the native woman shooing him away as he hesitates to leave my presence. As he trots off, I put away all desire for the boy dog and turn my attention on the woman. I have not drunk this night and she will pay by satisfying my thirst.

Unafraid, she stands waiting under the full light of the moon. I hesitate to attack or even to approach her until I can gauge her strength and ability. The idea comes that she might wait the night away and then, when I am weakened by the day, put an end to me. I have to kill her now while I have the strength. The woman is a threat as well as a food source. I step forth into the moonlight. Will she regard such a slight female as a threat? We confront each other. There is something threatening about her inactivity, but what can a savage do to me? She does not even carry a weapon, but then there was the light that seared my arm. I can still feel the pain and there are the blisters on my skin. I need blood to fully effect a cure.

I examine the sturdy native woman before me. She is black with the broad features and snub noses of these natives. Her hair is cut short, but roughly as if it has been hacked off, and she stands there naked and unashamed. Everything is revealed to my gaze. Her heavy breasts with their brown nipples lying upon her chest and above them the raised welts of three ill-healed scars. Her hips are broad and her belly bears the stretchmarks of birthing. She has powerful thighs, but thin shanks, and her pubic hair is dark and curly in the vee of her groin. I let my eyes feast on her luxuriance and, in spite of myself, my fangs emerge as I contemplate sucking up the blood that courses with such force along her veins and arteries.

She stares back at me steadily and suddenly I feel ashamed. My frame appears small and fragile, but this is part of my weaponry for no one might ascertain the strength I possess. Now her eyes examine me in turn and again the feeling of shame arises. I was once a decent girl and now am attired worse than the worst slattern. I wear only a thin white shift all soiled and bloodstained. Of course, when I boarded upon the ship I was clothed more decorously, though a trifle flamboyantly as suited my supposed profession, but the long months of the voyage during which I lurked in the hidden depths of the vessel, knowing only darkness, the creaking of timbers, the feel of male bodies and the taste of both their bloods turned me into a thing of coarseness as rough and uncaring of appearance as any of my prey. Now her eyes are on my blonde hair. My right hand reaches up to feel its knots and tangles. Indeed, I have become a sailor's drab, dirty and bedraggled. My skin is soiled and despoiled with their touch and blood. I need a long and pleasant bath to wash away all the grime of that confined existence. I need to have those things so that I may pass as a decent woman again. I stare at the savage before me and shudder, for if I do attain to a degree of civilised living I will become as this creature before me. It is then that I realise I must go to the settlement and regain what I feel I am about to lose.

Suddenly I find a voice speaking in my mind. The native woman has the gift too and worse she is feeling pity for me. She says, 'I don't know what you are or how you came to be here, but leave me and my own alone.'

I decide on subterfuge and, clasping my wounded arm, I moan aloud. I am careful not to project into her mind for I do not want her to know that I too possess the gift.

'You puny thing,' she feels and I exult in her images for they convey to me that she knows not what I am or what danger I can present, though her next projections make me wary of her and her power. 'I hurt you, but you ghost things are too often deadly to us humans. You come on all weak and helpless and then turn on us. I did not want to harm you, but I had to protect my son. Now let me have a look at that wound.'

Hiding my glee, I give utterance again to a mournful moan while sinking to the ground, a poor pitiful girl, almost a child, as she comes to me. She bends over me and cannot help exclaiming in both her mind and mouth her reaction to me. 'Phew, what a smell. How rank you are, but there is a pool close by. If that dirt is not washed from your wound, it'll be the end of you, though that might be a good thing.'

She takes my slight form in her arms, again evincing pity. I let her lift me. I even rest my head upon her breast, aping a weakened state. This evokes strong feelings within her, maternal feelings, that affect me too and weaken my resolve to partake of her blood. Somewhat helpless and confused in her arms, I let her carry me towards the pool where my dog, her son, had ripped the animal apart. There she puts me down and pulls off my shift. I stand as naked as she, though I am but a slight pale shadow beside her. I feel even my cheeks burning, for I had had instilled in me from an early age the impropriety of being completely unclothed. No person, except my mother, had ever seen me naked, and even in the worst conditions I have clung to my sense of modesty, as precious an ornament as the other. After all that I have been through and done, I am still a virgin. And so I stand, bashfully drooping in front of her until she tugs me into the water. Her rough but gentle hands begin scrubbing me with scoops of river mud. She washes me all over and then tries to untangle and unknot my hair, though as she has no comb or brush this is not successful. I let the woman tug and pull for I feel a curious contentment in at last being taken care of. Her hands soothe me and as she examines my wound, her heavy breast falls against my arm. I feel a vein throbbing there and a raging thirst replaces any tender feelings. I will have her. Now she plasters mud over my wound and I let her, though it will be healed by the morrow.

I let her take me from the water and lean against her as if in weakness still. How strong and how rich her blood will be. I feign a sudden fainting spell and sink to the ground at her feet. She bends to lift me to my feet or to take me in her arms to carry me. Whatever her intention, I have mine. I leave off all pretence and as my face comes up I sink my fangs into her neck. Her rich red fluid gushes into my mouth. At last I have her and I will suck her dry.

Suddenly I gag, push myself out from her arms and vomit. Her blood reeks of the sea and is harsh like fish oil. Visions of my mother giving me cod liver oil come into my mind and I retch again and again.

'You're one of those blood suckers,' the woman says within my mind. 'Well, my blood is too strong for you. Now what am I to do with such a devil?'

She reaches down and pulls me to my feet, imprisoning me in her strong arms. 'And such a little thing too. What happened to you, child?

Maybe ...'

She does not know the strength I possess. I break free of her arms and run for my life. I, the hunter, now feel the pangs of the prey. I blunder through the wood and out onto the plain then rush towards the only place I can think of in my panic, the cave. In the sky above me, I hear the flap-flap of fleshy wings and might have cowered in fright if my legs, under their own direction, were not propelling me towards what I hope will be a place of safety. A huge thing swoops over me and there is a rush of air that truly does make me cower. I know that I am done for, that now it is my turn to have my blood drained. She is similar to me and must have the same tastes. I, the mistress of the hunt, have become prey, destined to be perhaps a servant of a savage or simply to cease to be.

I close my eyes as the thing lands. The footsteps of the native woman sound as she comes towards my quivering body. I wait for what is to come. A hand touches me, then leaves.

'Just leave me and my own alone,' she images in my mind. 'Just leave us alone and I'll let you go, you poor helpless thing.'

And she is gone, leaving me quivering with anger rather than panic. Not even worthy to be prey. How could she spurn me so; how could she render me into a simpering thing worthy only of her pity? I get to my feet and stare up into the night sky at the receding shape of a giant bird or other creature. Some of these natives have strange and awful powers which equal or surpass my own. I cannot remain alone in the bush. It would be putting myself in peril. I walk back towards the cave and suddenly realise that I am still naked, though without shame. I return to the pool and find my shift and wash it out. I put on the wet and clinging garment. Now I will make my way to the settlement and rejoin my fellow countrypeople. Amongst them I will be safe, and to ease my thirst I can make forays out into the countryside. But should I take my box? No. For the time being, it must remain in the cave. I send out a message to my servant, Renfiel. I need him for my plan to escape this wilderness and effect entry into the settlement.

CHAPTER TEN

Captain Torrens felt that he had suffered a great defeat with the death of five of his men, especially the sergeant whom he had relied on to keep order, at least when he was near enough to make sure that some semblance of discipline was maintained. All of them had been drunk and appeared to have put up not the slightest resistance. He would never have allowed himself to be taken off guard. He cursed the sergeant again for not exerting his authority.

When he had arrived back at the wreck of the *Kore* with the carts, he had expected to find the detachment ready to load up. The sergeant was nowhere in sight and neither were the soldiers under him. He had roundly cursed the sergeant for what seemed to be a personal act of betrayal, then stared at the scene of desolation. His shout for them to come at the double was shrill and thin. They had not obeyed his order. He had glared around and his scowl came to rest on the pathetic remains of the vessel, stranded upon the land with her cargo spewing out across the shallows and the beach for anyone to plunder.

'Such a good ship,' he had murmured. 'Such a waste that we can ill afford,' he said to his second-in-command, a Lieutenant Plover who was just as weak and ill-disciplined as the rest. He had moved his scowl to the mutilated bodies of the natives hanging all in a row. A horde of black flies feasted on them.

'Sir, those savages, shouldn't they be given some sort of burial? The stench is terrific and there is no cologne water.'

The Captain's face had darkened and twisted even more and his forehead had furrowed. 'It is what the murderous scum deserve. Their stink will drive away any who try to pilfer our stores. If I had had the men to surround all the blighters, every man Jack of them would be hanging as a decoration to their foul handiwork. Now where are those damn men of mine? They were to guard the wreck. Hiding from the stink, I expect.' And he shouted, 'Fire a musket! A flogging will add to the romance of this desolate shore. The stinking savages hanging dead and the thud of the lash upon a deserter's flesh – what else could we do to realise this Gothic scene?'

The musket had been duly fired, but still the detachment failed to appear. 'Load up what supplies you can salvage quickly. I'll find them and then the sergeant will flog them, and after he is finished I'll flog him,' Torrens shouted at Lieutenant Plover.

Plover, whose gambling debts had necessitated him being away from the old country for a time, though not this far away, looked at the wreck. He tried to avoid seeing the carnage beside it, but he could not avoid the stench. He held a handkerchief to his nose as he gave the necessary orders, wishing that he had never thought that being under the command of Captain Torrens would be an easier course to take rather than facing the duns and the irritation of a father who had threatened to cut him off without a penny more times than he cared to recall.

Captain Torrens had scowled at Lieutenant Plover as he issued the appropriate orders and glowered at the men as they began collecting kegs and bales preparatory to loading them onto the carts. He had shouted to them to get a move on, then had stamped off to look for his missing men.

He was not always the irascible commander who dealt out more floggings than issues of rum. It was only at certain times of the month that he felt definitely out of sorts and it was then that the slightest thing set him off. These periods of heightened emotions began to peak towards the full moon and the taciturn, often indolent Captain became a demon ready to pounce upon the slightest infringement of army discipline. Instead of allowing things to take their course, as he did when the moon was waning so that discipline suffered and standards slipped, he tried to stamp his mark on his small force and make his men soldierly in bearing and manner. Such desires for military order and discipline peaked at full moon, as did his binges which were the whisper of the regiment and the terror of the neighbours and towns in which it had been stationed. Strange murders and even stranger sightings had occurred and often the dishevelled state of the Captain together with the discovery of yet another mutilated body became the talk of the mess. Rumour-mongers suggested that both occurrences were linked, but any such talk had to be spoken well beyond the ear of the Captain who, when once his honour had been impugned by a fellow officer, had challenged and then fought a duel with sabres in which he had, in a berserker's rage, killed his man. It was only with great difficulty that the affair had been laid to rest, but the resulting reputation of ferocity which the Captain had earned kept his fellow officers on their best behaviour when he was in their company. Captain Torrens was a misanthrope and eventually things would have gone badly for him had he not been given this posting, where it was thought that he might do little harm.

Now, with the moon in the ascendancy and his mood peaking, Torrens swore that he would award himself with the sound of the lash on flesh and the sight of blood being drawn for being put to the trouble of locating those he already saw as 'deserters'. It did not enter his mind that they might have come to grief, for he believed his treatment of the savages had been horrible enough to keep them away from the beach at least until the bodies rotted away. Of course, it was only to be expected that the mutinous sods would get into the rum, but for that they would pay. He did not expect to find what he now did. Thus he was startled enough to forget to scowl when he came across the body of the first soldier in a vee between two sand dunes. The soldier's fired musket lay beside him and his throat had been ripped open with such savagery that his head had almost been severed from his body. Torrens cocked his pistol and continued to search. He came across three others, including the sergeant who had shared the same fate. His scowl returned as he stared at the bodies, trying to imagine the ferocity of the onslaught. His mood was such that he enjoyed the massacre rather than being repelled by it.

'Silly buggers,' he growled, his lips twisting into an animal snarl as he focussed on the dead sergeant.

He went on and found their camp, the remaining soldier and the broached keg of rum. He picked up a pannikin and dipped it into the keg. He swished the contents around, then flung them at the dead face of the soldier. 'Well, one less for the lash,' he snarled, refilling the mug and draining it. Pensively he stared at the long spear piercing the man's neck and pinning him to the ground. 'That surely hurt more than any lashes I might have ordered,' he said harshly, carefully examining the signs of how the unfortunate wretch had scrabbled about as his life drained from his body. 'It's what a soldier's life is all about,' he snarled again as he refilled his pannikin and lifted it in a wry toast. 'Here's to rum, sodomy, the lash and a soldier's death,' he declared, then tossed off the drink and flung the mug down.

The Captain returned to the beach in a mood made even fouler by the fiery spirit. He cursed the men to hurry up and load the carts. 'Damn it, the bloodthirsty savages have been at their dastardly work again, so get a move on,' he shouted. 'Christ! When we are all secure, I'll make them rue the day they came against me. Now hurry, load the damn carts. We'll send boats from the settlement for the rest. Now two of you come with me, I have work for you to do. I'll hex them yet.'

His orders were almost always passed down the chain of command so when he gave a direct order, the men hung back in trepidation. He pointed at two soldiers and without a further word left the beach. The men followed after him, forgetting to take their muskets though he had not expressly ordered it, and the lieutenant looking after them hesitated to add to the order, for he knew the moods of his commander and though he was not under the threat of the lash, who knew what action the Captain might take if he deigned to alter or amend his direct command.

When the two soldiers came across the bodies they were almost paralysed with fear. 'Pick that one up and take him to the top of that dune,' the Captain ordered. The men stared at each other. 'See this pistol? By the time I cock it, I want that body up there.'

Their fear of the Captain won out and with alacrity they obeyed his commands. They did the same with the other corpses, one of which was without its scarlet jacket.

'Now I want them tied in place. Stake them in a sitting-up position. Get some pieces of wood from the wreck!'

The two soldiers hurried off. While they were gone, the Captain had another rum as he finalised his plans. When the men returned with pieces of spar, he ordered them to lash the dead men to the stakes. He examined the sitting-up figures and had lengths of wood placed in their hands so that from a distance they seemed to be holding muskets.

'That should keep the savages from the wreck,' the Captain grimaced. 'You two, a mug of rum for both of you. Now tip the keg over.'

They returned to the beach to find that the three carts, all that the settlement possessed, were fully loaded. When the two soldiers had returned for the lengths of wood, they had whispered about the massacre of their comrades to the others, elaborating on the spear in the throat of one and the hideous wounds of the others to such an extent that the panic-stricken soldiers rushed to finish their work so that they could get back to the safety of the settlement.

Their Captain's treatment of their comrades' bodies on another occasion and in a different locality might have caused a mutiny. But this time there was scarcely a murmur of protest raised as the laden carts made off along the beach.

'We'll send the boats for the rest of it,' Torrens said, glowering at Lieutenant Plover. 'One boat'll stand off the beach and if a savage shows himself for an instant, that one'll be dead and strung up with the others. I'll show them what savagery is. Now march. Double step, you lot. We have to get back to the settlement just in case the natives try to overrun it. Who knows,' he snarled, though without acknowledging his responsibility, 'with our whole force here they might already be among the civilians. Imagine the slashing and hacking, the blood running and then the cooking up of the bodies as they get ready to tuck into them. "Long pig", they are said to call it in the South Sea Islands,' he informed his men with relish, watching from his nag as they rushed to help the carts through the sand and onto firmer ground.

The settlement was a half day's journey from the scene of the wreck and was built on the middle of a peninsula jutting out from the eastern side of a long sweeping bay. At the western edge was a long narrow indentation which ran inland for a number of miles and necessitated a long detour for the carts and marching men. Captain Torrens, under threat of attack from bloodthirsty savages, revelled in the situation. He sent ahead an advance party and then formed a rear guard. The main body, if it could be called that for the force was small, consisted only of the three carts and their drivers. Lieutenant Plover thought that any determined attack might break the column into three, but a glance at the scowling face of his superior officer stopped him from asking if such precautions were really wise or even necessary.

The landscape, except for a few birds, lay bare and deserted. The sky for once was clear, though on the southern horizon hovered masses of cloud which might or might not herald another tempest. No smoke from campfires streaked the pellucid blue above, and the only sounds were those of their passage, a few rustles in the undergrowth and the cawing of a crow which inquisitively swung over the convoy and even perched on one of the carts until the driver's curses and whip drove it protesting up into the branches of a storm-battered tree. The creaking of the cartwheels, the cracks of whips, the dragging hooves of horses not in the best condition and the shuffling boots of dejected men sounded like a detachment of Napoleon's army on its retreat from Moscow. Many of the soldiers were indeed veterans of the French wars and knew what it was like to run with their tails between their legs. All of them hated the dangerous position they were in and blamed their commander for it. He though, perhaps imagining himself a Marshal Ney, the hero of that terrible retreat, was filled with a nervous energy which kept him riding from vanguard to rear. Perforce the lieutenant had to follow suit, although it tired the horses and if they were lamed in this vacant land where could others be found to replace them; but again the lieutenant kept his peace.

'Hey, lads, how about a song to move your marching feet,' Captain Torrens shouted all at once, with such a snarl that the men stopped their shuffle. '*The Deserter*, lads, that'll be the one.'

The best voice in the group took up the song in a quavering voice which the others added to:

> *In fair London city I was born,*
> *And for a soldier I was drawn;*
> *A kidnapping sergeant on me did prevail,*
> *And he hoisted me down to the savoy jail.*

'Step lively, men and shout those words so that you'll scare away any savage lying in ambush.' The Captain's encouragement only served to lessen the singing. Savagely, he took up a verse:

> *O then a court martial they did call,*
> *And I was brought before them all;*
> *My sentence was past – I was not to be shot,*
> *But a thousand lashes was to be my lot.*

It was then that the convoy turned around the edge of the fjord and entered onto the peninsula which was rough and rocky so that the men had to bend their backs to the wheels. Captain Torrens cursed them on then, not bothering to wait with them, galloped off towards the settlement.

The settlers had decided that they had little to fear from the natives for what was a rude spear against a musket ball, but since the news of the massacre of the ship's crew, anxiety had swept the little settlement. Under the direction of the Government Resident, a palisade was being constructed across the narrowest section of the peninsula and it was towards this that Captain Torrens turned his attention as he galloped in. He stopped in front of the Resident, Mr Mathews and shouted with positive glee, 'They slaughtered five of my best men the other night. They're on the war path and will be down on us in no time. See these gaps in this fence – a greasy savage could slither through and slit your throat, like they did my men and the crew of the *Kore*. Worse, they're cannibals and you'll be roasting over the cooking fire in no time. They reckon long pig is the best meat of all.' He gave a harsh laugh.

'Sir,' remonstrated Mr Mathews, 'there is no need to spread alarm. No need at all. This fence, I mean palisade, is well under way and when strengthened will protect us from any naked savages.'

'That's what my men thought,' declared the Captain. 'Their throats were ripped out, sir. Their blood drunk all up, sir. Palisade indeed. This fence they will jump if they cannot slither through,' and he grimaced and galloped off to his house. He flung himself off the nag, leaving it to be stabled by one of his men, and stamped into the house where his wife waited in trepidation for she knew well what to expect when the moon waxed full. His moods then often resulted in terrible assaults that no decent woman, though she might bear them, could mention in company. They had steadily grown worse since they had arrived and set up house at the desolate outpost. There was no escaping him except by retreating further and further into a listless state which dulled her senses, though it made him mistreat her the more.

She cowered in the rough kitchen when she heard the sound of his horse's hooves and by the time he stamped in she had a plate of hash on the table. It was the very dregs of the bottom of the barrel of salt beef, but she dared not broach his newly arrived supplies without permission. He flung his hat at her, then his coat and slumped at the table, taking up a fork to raise a sample of the food to his mouth. He poked it in through his sardonic lips, then called, 'Jane!'.

She left off hanging up his coat and hastened to him,. She had been ready to brush it as he had ordered often enough before, but she knew what would happen if she hesitated.

'And what is this?' he asked sternly, gesturing at the plate as if it contained a mass of worms. 'I might not have married you for your looks, but at least I thought that you could cook.' He picked up the plate and hurled it into her face. Grimacing with distaste, he watched her reel away. Such a mousy woman whose once passable looks had faded. She had come with a thousand pounds and he had taken her for that.

'Clean up that ugly face of yours, you slut,' he snarled at her. 'And might you not make an effort to please me? I do not like your hair in a bun, let it flow free; and as for that dress, that sack if I may call it so, it has seen better days. It is as dowdy as your features. Now get me a bottle of wine. At least I managed to get a chest sent from London and there are those jars of caviar also newly arrived. Bring them and depart. Try to make yourself presentable as befits the wife of a Captain of the Royal Army by the time I return. I go to see to my laggards before I attend to you.' He rose to his feet and flung the fork at her, then waited while she brought his coat and hat before stamping off.

Jane broke into a fit of trembling, every shouted command from outside setting her off again. Eventually his voice receded from her ears and she became settled enough to locate the wine and caviar. After, she drew a bath and washed her body under her shift as best she could in the tepid water. She went to her trunk and discovered that the moths had feasted on most of the clothing she had carried with her to this land. There was the faded satin of her wedding dress. She took it out and held it against her. Once she had worn it with pride and had stood before the altar with the handsome Captain. Her parents had been content with the match and they little knew, nor did she, what lay in store for her. The handsome Captain was a monster and, unlike other army officers with a passion for cards, wine or women, he had other and more sinister vices which had soon reduced her to a drudge. She sighed and pulled the dress over her head while stepping out of the damp shift. She hated to see even a part of her body. Once she had been plump with a fine figure; now she was a scarecrow and the dress fell about her like a shroud, but there was little else to wear and she lacked the urge to attempt to please him. She buttoned up the dress then combed out her hair. Once it had been lustrous, thick and dark but now was thin and greying and it hung about her pallid face like string. She shrugged, then went and huddled in the kitchen, letting the tears fall and her shrunken bosom heave as she mourned her life.

CHAPTER ELEVEN

How I long for the sun to sink, for the day is cursed with too much light and I must skulk here at the back of the cave with nothing to distract me but memories of last night and Renfiel and the strangeness of his instrument. I trust that he will prove a faithful servant, though he has little say in the matter when I have the wherewithal to entice him and the power to keep him captive. He supped on my blood and I on his and now he shall come when I call. Though he has not a word of my tongue, this does not matter, for even a dog learns to obey the slightest command of his mistress – and I shall have my dog too soon. This causes me to think of the woman and of her vigilance and power. She knows my hiding place and seeks to protect her whelp, but in time I shall feast again on him, then decide if he too shall be a servant or just cold drained clay. Now I feel the evening close, waiting to enter as the sun prepares to depart. He drops over the horizon and the moon replaces him. She is full and cool on my body as I stand at the entrance calling Renfiel to me. I have need of his hands and he can guide me to the settlement where I shall not be denied a refuge.

He comes, limping slowly towards me. He does not want to be here for he has some other business with his fellows, but that will have to wait as he will carry my sacks of earth. I still hesitate over my box. Should I take it or leave it here? I shall leave it, for perhaps the settlement will not be as safe as I think it to be. There is a being of a monstrous passion there, waiting to reach fulfilment with the rising of the full moon. We are much alike, for we have similar persuasions and I can reach out to enter his mind without the necessary exchange of blood. He waits impatiently for the change to come so that he can go hunting. This night he intends to rampage through the bush, inflicting a bloody vengeance on the natives as he blames them for my petty crimes. The blood of his soldiers lacked substance, too poor and tainted from the rum they had imbibed to go down well with me. Still, I quenched my thirst with them and have no need to sup just yet. Now here stands my trusty servant, or should I call him slave and elevate myself by so doing to the level of those noble ladies who paraded with such as he in the old country? No matter, slave or servant means the same and I command instant obedience.

He picks up my bags of earth. I place within his mind the image of what I imagine the settlement to be like. The captain, my sister's husband, before he was drained of all vitality and cast aside as an empty husk had described in miserable detail the isolation and poverty of the outpost flung upon these shores. He had been contracted to supply it, and the money was little enough to encourage his pilfering of what stores he could which he sold at the Cape Colony. I had no need to pilfer, and soon neither did he. Now my trusty servant limps in front of me. He has an amusing gait and physique. I stare at his bare arse poking out from underneath the military jacket he has stolen and smile. It is because I find him quaint that I will let him live on until he ceases to entertain me. I mimic his walk for some steps, then grow weary and take to the skies. My leathern wings catch the breeze and I soar high, exulting in my freedom. I swoop down upon some .hapless animal and sample its blood. Eucalyptus does give a tang to their vital fluid. Now I dart over the fence that separates the settlement from the mainland. It is a barrier meant to prevent intruders from entering. I close my wings and come to the ground. Two soldiers are on guard. They stare uneasily beyond the fence, and into the shadows raised by the moonlight, then get together to smoke a pipe. So easy, I could have them in a thrice, but it is then that the dangerous one stalks to them and shouts for them to be aware. It is then that I resolve to have him before his change occurs. I exult in the savagery that is surging in his blood, demanding release. The potency of his vital fluid makes me squeak and I almost lose my shape. I take to the sky and his eyes jerk up to me.

'A giant bat, sir,' one of the soldiers shouts. 'Shall I bring it down?'

He lifts his musket, but the brute knocks it away. 'You fool,' he brays, 'the settlement is edgy enough as it is without you firing at some damn bat. If you want to try your prowess use one of those long native spears. Get used to the feel before you find it in your throat.' And he stamps away as I dart away back to my servant who is just limping onto the peninsula. I land, change back and walk beside him. I will use him in my plan to effect entry into the settlement. There is the gate now, and there are the two guards, driven apart by their brutish commander but edging together again for support against the terrors of the night. I taste their fear, but it is not enough for them to ignore a young woman in distress.

'Help me, please help me,' I call out plaintively.

'Who's there?' one of the soldiers calls, his musket coming up and his finger going to the trigger.

'Please help me,' I call again.

'Stay where you are,' he shouts.

His comrade exclaims, 'It's a trick of those savages.'

His voice is a nervous whisper, but my keen ears hear him and I respond. 'No, no,' I cry, 'I am from the *Kore*. Thank God, thank God,' and

I begin sobbing and laughing altogether as if in hysterics.

They are not taken in entirely by my wiles. In truth I did not expect them to be, but what I did expect now comes to pass. 'Better get the Cap'n,' one says to the other. 'He's the one to deal with this.'

Long moments pass broken only by my sobbing. Now the Captain comes and shouts, 'Who are you!'

'Sir, sir,' I cry, then pass back into my wild sobbing.

'Enough of that damn sobbing. Show yourself or get a ball,' he shouts.

I feel the energy surging through his body in waves. How he must strive to keep himself human. I step out into the moonlight where he can see me, then urge Renfiel to do the same. We stand there while he examines us.

'Make your way to the gate,' he finally calls. 'Both of you. Our guns are on you. Just remember I hate savages.'

Such is his threat, but I notice how his voice softens a fraction when he eyes me, then it hardens again as his gaze encounters my native servant and his red coat. To ease any suspicion, Renfiel has dropped my sacks in the shadow of a boulder so that we are bereft of anything which might be construed as a weapon. Empty-handed we stand at the gate. A soldier unfastens it and we pass through. I have breached their defences. Now, see if they can expel me. Immediately I fling myself at the feet of their Captain, seemingly in heartfelt gratitude. My arms go about his knees and my face presses against him close to his groin. I feel him stir as I upturn my tearstained face and sad eyes to wail, 'My Blessed Lord has heard my prayers and answered them. Sweet Saviour, I am saved. Good sir, I am a survivor of the *Kore*. It would have gone terribly for me but for this noble savage. He, at great peril to his own self, hid me away from his bloodthirsty kind.'

The Captain scowls down at me, then scowls across at the native. 'Guard him,' he orders, 'he has on an army jacket. Now, how came you to be on the ship?' he asks me.

'Sir, I am the wife of the captain of the poor vessel, Eliza Fraser, and ...' I break into sobs again and press my face against his thigh.

'Yes, yes,' he says impatiently. He is more moved by my proximity than by my distress. In fact, that does not interest him at all. 'Well, come with me and I'll hear your story later. The native can come too. I'll chain him at my door. No, he did help you. You two, take this savage and fling him outside the fence. If he is not gone in a minute, shoot him!'

Renfiel is pushed through the gate and scampers off, happy to get away so lightly. Perhaps he should be punished for this act of desertion, but if he *had* stayed I would have lost a servant, for this brute hates these people and might dispatch him without a qualm, especially with the change on him. Now he turns from the soldiers on guard, bends down and pulls me to my feet. I come up, feigning a weakness, and lean against him so that he must place an arm about me. He needs little urging, especially as he can feel the fullness of my breast against his side. During the months on the boat I have drunk well and often and my body has filled out as much as my physique permits. My cheeks, under their smearing of the dust I covered them with, might also be seen to be too rosy for one who has suffered much, being the single survivor of a wrecked vessel and the unwilling observer of the massacre by savages of an entire ship's complement.

His body and mind are racked by the rising moon. Impatiently he drags me towards his house, one of the better two in the settlement, which is as miserable as the captain of the *Kore* described to me as he added to its wretchedness by selling off a goodly portion of the supplies destined for it. He pushes me through into the front room of the house which is as ill-furnished as any hovel in the slums of London. A sad drudge of a woman slinks away from us to a corner where she sits on a stool. She is wearing a faded and stained satin wedding dress and her bedraggled hair and general appearance remind me of my own lack of furbishment.

Suddenly, as if only then realising the immodesty of my partially clad form, I huddle on the couch which is the best piece of furniture in the room, wrap my arms across my breasts and murmur bashfully, 'Sir, sir, I have been adrift in the wilderness with only that savage for company. I am covered with dirt and lack clothes and ...' I begin to wail and blubber, 'I have lost all. My dear husband and my chest of clothing. Sir, when the ship first struck the reef I was asleep and came on deck just as you see me in this shameful state. I would have dressed but then the waves impetuously flung the doomed vessel onto the beach. I was thrown into the water, then they came ... savages ...' and I affect a breakdown, flinging myself in a paroxysm of grief against him, my benefactor, who clasps me in his strong arms.

'You are indeed somewhat rank,' he says gruffly, though this does not put him off for I feel him stirring against me. 'A bath, yes, a bath, that is what you need,' he says, as the blood rushes to his face and his arms tighten about me. 'Jane', he shouts, 'hot water. Jane, prepare a bath in the kitchen for the lady. Get to it now!'

The woman scurries off to obey him while I remain in his arms, pressed against his chest. He mentioned my rankness; well, his is just as strong. An animal fetidness emanates from his body and is almost enough to make me forget myself, not through repulsion but through attraction. His entire frame is flooded with a vitality which makes me long to sink my fangs into the heavy vein that pulsates at the side of his neck. Beyond myself, my mouth opens just as he pushes me away and examines me at arm's length. Hastily I lower my face.

'Yes, yes, such a calamity. One which must be avenged again and again. Jane,' he shouts, 'this poor victim needs to be decently clad. Search through your trunk and let you come up with something with which she may cover herself. Then she needs brushes for her hair and food for her stomach. She must be as famished as I am.'

The woman must be hard at work in the kitchen for she makes no reply. This sets him off. He thrusts me roughly down upon the couch and stamps off to the kitchen. There is the sound of a blow, then feverish sounds of the bath being prepared. Now he returns and leads me into the kitchen. The woman is filling a tub with hot water.

'Jane,' he orders, 'this poor woman needs to be bathed. Her ordeal has weakened her. Bathe and clothe her, then see to her toilette for her hair is all entangled. It needs to be combed and dressed for beneath that grime she is devilishly attractive.'

He takes up a bottle of wine, glances at me as if ready to offer me a drink, thinks better of it and goes into the other room. The woman hovers around me, or rather shrinks around me, for the poor dear has little spirit left in her. I stare at her and her eyes turn towards the floor. I continue to gaze until her complexion assumes a muddy cast. Her blood, I know, would be a pallid fluid not worth the taking.

'Where is the clothing?' I demand, noticing how she gives a start when she hears my words. 'I cannot go around like this,' I add, running my hands over my body. Indeed the thin chemise I have on is not for decency or even fit for seduction as it is so soiled, though the brutish Captain seems to have liked what it revealed.

'Where do you go to when you need to see to your bodily functions?' I ask the woman.

She indicates the back door with a nod. She is slow to open it. I do it for myself and step outside, then turn and tell the drab, 'I'll go by myself while you see to my attire. Nothing indecorous,' I add with a smile, knowing that the poor drab would have little with regard to costumes of allure. Before she can answer, that is if she intended to for all the words have been long beaten out of her, I close the door behind me and look over the compound. The moon floods it with light, but even at this time of evening there are few about, and these are clustered about the cooking fires which burn in front of their makeshift shelters. I stare towards the only other dwelling of note on the far side of the compound and at the very lip of the peninsula. I turn from it as I have no business there as yet, then in order to remain concealed I assume my bat shape and take to the air, startling a crow which gives an undignified squawk as he flops off. Another time the bird might have provided me with sport, especially as I feel that there is something about it which needs investigating, but I am in a hurry and must be back at the house before my absence is noticed. I reach the fence and silently circle it. The two soldiers are at the gate and visible from the Captain's dwelling. I feel no eyes upon me as I land on the ground and assume my human shape.

'Sirs, I regret that I did not thank you for saving me from my perilous situation,' I say softly, starting the two who have been squatting on their haunches and sharing a pipe.

They spring up and eye me. I stay where I am and smile at them. I can feel that they have not had the benefit of female company for many months and their eyes sweep over my form barely concealed by the chemise.

'Nothing to it, miss,' one of them says. Both of them move closer to me and thus out of sight of the windows of the Captain's house. 'We hesitated a little, but if you had seen what those savages had done ...' He stops in embarrassment, for he had quite forgotten that I, as the sole survivor, would have seen it all. 'I'm sorry, miss,' he blurts out, 'but there comes to an old soldier a feeling in the air just like before a battle, you know ...'

'Yes, I know,' I exclaim and stepping up to him I snap his neck, then that of his comrade.

Such a simple procedure and now I open the gate, not even hesitating to watch the struggle of their souls to leave their expiring bodies. I run to the boulder where Renfiel deposited my bags of earth, easily lift them and hasten back. Within the fence I stare down at the two soldiers, watching their last tremors with interest. Now I must make this the work of the savages. I get on my hands and knees and extend my fangs. I plunge them into the neck of the first soldier and feel the hot blood spurt into my mouth. I lap it up before ripping the throat out of my victim, and now it is the turn of the other one. This one I extend my prowess on, ripping open his trousers and relieving him of his manhood, again with my fangs so that I may taste and sample his blood. I stuff his organ into his mouth and, taking up my sacks, glide back to the Captain's dwelling.

The drab hardly notices my return; her vacant grey eyes barely glance up at my entrance. Somewhat annoyed by this lack of attention, for my recent repast has reddened my lips and chin and indeed has spurted over the front of my shift, I come close to her so that she can see the traces of the red fluid distinctly, even though the light in the kitchen comes only from the coals of the fire. It is to this lack of illumination that I attribute the absence of terror in her eyes, for in such a light the rich ruby red of blood becomes only a dark stain. Thus I am not over.ly concerned about her lack of response, and now remove my shift without the shame I would lately have felt, giving her the opportunity to view my form which is glowing from my recent repast. It receives barely a glance as, naked as the day I was born, I step into the tin tub and lower myself into the warm water.

'Now come, I need your assistance to wash me all over,' I tell the woman. She kneels down beside the tub and picking up a stub of soap begins my ablutions. Her hands are rough on my skin, but I am not aroused, even when she bends her head and her hair sweeps to one side to show her white neck. I smile and reveal my fangs in amusement, for the jugular vein is barely pulsing and the fluid within would taste of vinegar if not of water.

'Now my hair,' I order her brusquely. 'It has become entangled and needs the greatest care taken with it. It is thick and a beautiful colour, is it not?' I ask her, trying to get some response. Again there is none, except her hands on my head, soaping my hair and seeking to untangle the knots and snarls. As she works I take a look at her face; it is vacant of the present. It is as if she has retreated into a past period when she had washed other hair as thick and lovely as my own. Perhaps the thinning and greying hanks which hang about her face were once as lustrous as mine? I examine the careworn face, detecting signs of what once was, if not beauty, then attractiveness. It is then that I feel a tinge of sorrow, or should I say compassion, for her. Some creatures should not be abused and she is one of them. I tell her that when I end her life it will be a clean kill, and she understands for tears begin to fall from her eyes. She seems not to notice them and they continue even when I am out of the bath and she is drying me with some rough cloth. They continue to fall while she carefully combs out my hair until it hangs free about my face.

I feel enlivened and hungry again when my toilette is finished. My feeling of wellbeing does not diminish even when I am put into a dress which does little to render me attractive. If I was in London, I would spurn such a rag with my foot and cast it out into the street. Still, it is brown and will hide any stains that might come upon it.

Now washed and dressed I make my appearance in the other room where I find the brute sitting at the table, an empty bottle of wine in front of him. He glances at me with an unholy gleam in his eye. The transformation is about to begin. I feel his whole physical being surging with cellular changes.

'Jane,' he shouts, 'another bottle of wine.'

The drab enters the room with downcast eyes and places the bottle before him.

'Another glass, if there is one remaining unbroken from your ineptitude,' he snarls at her. His fingers shoot out and fasten on her arm. She winces and I see an expression of sheer terror shift her features. She is well aware of his approaching transformation and the result of it. His steely grip, which has left the bruised marks of indentation in her arm, is but a foretaste of what she can expect from the brute overwhelmed by the powers of the full moon.

She returns with a dusty glass which he fills, then motions me to sit opposite to him. I do so with a smile.

'You, Jane, on your corner stool!'

Obediently, she goes and huddles in her corner.

The Captain regards me in silence. His burning eyes glide over me. I have to act and put an end to this menace.

'Sir,' I cry, 'sir, how can I repay you for saving me from those savages?'

'Well, perhaps you owe the saving to your own devices,' he replies sardonically, staring into my eyes as if reading the answer there. Such brutes as he are able to see beneath the cloak of seeming innocence and worse, he too might have the power to enter minds. Unease unfixes my resolve, but all that I can do is continue to play the victim. I open my mouth to declare my virginity when I recall that I am a widow lately bereaved and change my tune. 'Sir,' I sob, adding for good measure, 'my saviour! I am alone in this world and at the far ends of the earth. What am I to do? Who will be a protector of this poor widow who saw her husband butchered before her very eyes? Those savages, they, they ...' I break off and fling my hands up to my face to shield the smile which flutters over my lips.

'Yes, yes, what did you see?' he demands, his animal nature fully aroused and dousing any suspicion he might have entertained as a rational being. He gets to his feet and stamps about the room. He comes to a stop before the affrighted Jane, curses her for an ill-begotten drab, then approaches to stand over me. Timidly I look up at him. I feel the brutal magnetism of his presence. I feel the cells mutating in rapid succession as the change begins.

'I could never describe their cruelties,' I sob out. I get to my feet and fling myself at his. 'Sir, my saviour, what am I to do now? What am I to do, alone in this land without kith or kin?'

His hands grip me and drag me up. I allow myself to be drawn halfway up his body, then cling to his hips, burying my face into his thigh and then into his hard groin.

'Sir, advise me, help me,' I cry, suppressing a laugh, for I have regained my confidence. I reach out and imprison his hands in a loose grip which I can tighten when he reacts. Using one of my fangs delicately, I slit the front of his trousers and take his strong and virile member in my mouth. He grunts as I set to work and so heated is he that his white blood spurts copiously after mere seconds, but such a creature is he that he continues to be erect. I tighten my grip on his paws and fully engulf him and bite down. He gives a great bellow of pain and rage as my teeth meet together. Desperately he seeks to free himself from my grip only to find that my strength is the equal of his. I manage to hold him as I lap the life blood spurting from him. His body shifts and strains. The change comes over him but too late. His hands are now indeed paws, hairy and rough. I feel his body thickening and swelling towards the heavy furry shape of a bear. I let none of this distract me. His blood is an elixir filled with power. I gulp down the rich bear essence while I exult in his attempts to get free of me. I suck away his strength and it is the most wonderful experience I have yet had. I keep at him until the last drop is within me and I am bloated and replete. Sated, I let the werebear loose. His empty remains fall at my feet and the human form begins to reassert itself as the bear spirit leaves.

'There,' I say and turn to his wife who is as still as a statue, though her eyes are large and glowing in her pallid face. 'There,' I repeat again, 'the brute is dead and he was delicious.'

I get to my feet and go to her. 'Let me kiss you, for I have relieved you of your torment,' I say, taking her face in my hands and placing my bloody lips full on hers. 'There, taste your husband for the last time,' and I break her neck as if I were snapping a twig. 'There,' I say, 'I have relieved you of your other torment which was your life.'

It is then that I become aware of a confusion of voices from outside the dwelling. No one presumes to enter, perhaps owing to the fact that the rages of the beast – at least as a man – are too well known and no one dares to intrude. Quickly I wipe what blood I can from my mouth using the dress I am wearing. The brown colour does indeed obscure blood stains. That done, I give a piercing shriek and scream, 'The savages, the savages, save me!' I fall, lapsing down into an apparent swoon as the door springs open and my milch cows rush in to rescue me.

CHAPTER TWELVE

My father, Jangamuttuk, and the other men reverted to their traditional costume, discarding their ghost clothing and putting on their pubic mother-of-pearl shells. They refashioned their hair, greasing and covering their locks with red ochre. When they had finished, they did not look like the local blackfellows but like themselves. Wadawaka did the same, although he was from faraway Africa, but he had been adopted into our tribe and perhaps belonged to it more than I did. I hesitated to copy my kinsmen for I had been born and raised on the mission under Fada who regarded such near nakedness and decoration as a manifestation of savagery from which, as he stated again and again, it was his duty to wean us. The women were also under his lingering influence. He had harangued them the most. They kept on their ghost skirts as they had done at the previous ceremony. Jangamuttuk took a long look at them, then at me.

'Well, you might not be a man yet, but you are not a woman,' he commented and ordered me to rid myself of my ghost clothing. I did so reluctantly, feeling somewhat awkward in being almost completely naked. My body too was paler than those of my kinsmen and I stood out from them as much as they stood out from the locals.

'When the sun hisses and strikes you again and again,' my father stated, 'the paleness of your skin will turn dark from his bites and you'll look like a regular blackfellow.'

Regular blackfellows, however, was not what the locals considered us, for when they returned with Spirit Master limping at their head, it was to stare at us in suspicion. Spirit Master himself still wore his red jacket and reminded me of one of the ghost dancers in our ceremony. Perhaps it was this that made my father decide to try to talk to him about the situation, though he had scant regard for him. He began with the ghost or spirit settlement not so far away, a half day's journey we had heard, and said that it had to be destroyed not only physically but psychically. Spirit Master listened with a scowl on his face.

His ugly expression deepened and he knit his brows together, his hand coming up to twist at a hank of his thin beard. 'Yes, but how do we know that you are not spies?' he ground out, gnashing his teeth as his anger exploded.

'Keep that up and you'll break your fangs,' Jangamuttuk retorted, switching from negotiation to confrontation. He had taken the measure of the so-called Spirit Master and knew that if it came to a duel, his spears would be easily evaded.

'Look at your ways,' Spirit Master shouted. 'You call yourself blackfellows and cover your hair with red like blood and even the designs on your pubic coverings are different from ours. Far south is the land of giants who rule over their smaller subjects. It is said that some of these flee from that land on the shields of those giants and for all we know ...' he glared around at his mob for confirmation, 'for all we know, you might be spies of those that have invaded my land. Now we have those spirits on that peninsula and next – I can feel it – there will be an invasion of those huge monsters from the south and we will not be able to withstand them. They hunger for human flesh and it will be our flesh that they will be eating. Did you not say that you were from a southern island? Yes, you did!' He set himself up in a stance of challenge.

'We are from a southern island, and once there were giants there it is true,' Jangamuttuk replied, 'but we had strong shamans among our mob who turned them into mountains of stone, though there was one who still lived and moved. This last giant was difficult to be rid of. He not only ate up all the game in our country but when he was hungry he came for the men and women. The shamans got together and talked over what was to be done, for they found that they could not kill him outright but would have to resort to subterfuge. He was made of stone and could not be harmed by any of our weapons. They formed a plan. One of them became a huge kangaroo while the others dug a deep and wide pit. They came to the giant and said that they had food for him. He came at a run, leaving them far behind, or he would have except that the shamans knew how to fly and came before him. He reached the pit and saw the kangaroo cooking there. He jumped down and the kangaroo sprang aside and out. The shamans chanted spells to keep that giant down while they piled up logs and even whole trees. With their crystals, they then set that heap alight. The fire blazed up and after five days the giant became so hot that he exploded. Bits of him went all over the country and what remained of him there cooled to a huge boulder which can be seen to this day. Thus, we are not afraid of giants.' Jangamuttuk scowled, chewing his beard and eyeing the man.

'A likely story indeed,' Spirit Master retorted.

'There is a way to settle it,' Jangamuttuk said softly. With his toes he dug into the sand and felt for the spear he had hidden there. Gripping the haft between big and second toe, he jerked it up into the air and caught it. 'There is a way to settle this,' he repeated. 'This is my thigh spear. I have wounded many a man with it. The barb is especially cruel for those that it strikes. The last one screamed when I pulled it from his flesh. He was lame ever after, much like you are, but you still have one good leg and that will be my mark.'

Spirit Master muttered, grimaced and looked at his mob where he found little support. He softened his voice as he answered, 'I too have stories and a spear, but if what you say is true, how come you sailed on that shield which you have hidden behind the broken one?'

'It is how we came to your land, and perhaps we were brought to your shores for a purpose. We know how to deal with those ghosts or spirits. We need to hold a ceremony to open up the way to their land, then send them back to where they belong.'

'Ceremony, ceremonies!' Spirit Master cried. 'I have enough of them and need no others.' He ground his teeth furiously, but made no move to take up my father's challenge.

Jangamuttuk shrugged as his attention shifted to a crow which flopped down upon the ground a little beyond our two mobs. It gave a caw which turned into a chuckle as it began to shimmer and change. There stood the shaman Crow before us. He took a moment to settle himself, smoothing his beard with one hand and his topknot with the other, then said, 'All present and correct. Sometimes I feel that I might reform as beams of sunlight. Ho, Whale Singer, what are you up to now?'

'Whale Singer no longer; now I am Spirit Master,' was the surly reply.

'Well, perhaps Spirit Familiar might be the more correct term, but if you are what you have named yourself, there are plenty of those white-skinned spirits to kill. They are on your land and await your attention,' Waai commented slyly.

'I have done nothing for I have been waiting for you. Their camp is on the borders of both our lands and a common response is called for.'

'Yes, indeed, a common response. My mob is on the way. First we must conduct a joint ceremony to strengthen ourselves and weaken them. After that, we will attack.'

'And did you receive my message stick?' asked Spirit Master sourly. 'It concerned these strangers. You can vouch for them as they carried a safe conduct from you. I saved them from the ire of my mob, but it is difficult to know whether they are spies or not. They have a floating shield exactly like the one my magic drove onto the shore.'

'Powerful magic indeed. It is a pity that you could not protect those men you have sent on their way. I passed their spirits as I flew here.'

'They shall be revenged; but for now, are these strange blackfellows who they say they are?'

'They are indeed, though their shaman is of the Eaglehawk fraternity and does not trust us Crows. Still, he is a ceremonial leader – but not as strong as you are,' Crow replied, staring sardonically at Spirit Master. 'I see that you wear the pelt of one of those spirits and also have reconnoitred their settlement. In the night there are eyes and eyes see. I had to pass their camp and saw you at your work.'

'Spirit Master is not to be surprised, nor is he afraid of such spirits,' the man boasted. 'This pelt, I took from one of them. It contains powerful magic.'

'Yes, and we will add to its potency,' Crow said. 'Our ceremony will be strong indeed with you there. Now we must prepare the ground and for this I need your help. Between the sand dunes overseen by those who guard that place and must be pacified – we shall level out the sand and have our ceremony there.'

'But that broken shield is close by,' protested Spirit Master. 'If they return and find us there ...'

'They will not return as yet, and besides the ceremony is conducted at night and when darkness reigns they keep to their own place. Blood has been spilt there and it is there that you acquired your coat of blood.'

'It is a place that I have rendered harmless. It is right that we hold the ceremony where I triumphed over them.'

'So all is settled. Take your mob and build a ceremonial circle. It must be ready when my tribe arrives.'

Spirit Master limped past us and his mob followed in his wake. Crow looked after him and spat. 'Whale Singer, Spirit Master, better Spirit Appeaser. Such a braggart, but then he will play an important part in the ceremony, one which will suit him well. Know you that as my Dreaming animal I visited the camp of those white-skinned ones and saw him there? In company with a long and yellow-haired female who led him by his brain and his vanity. Yes, he has an important part to play and I have dreamt his costume already.'

'There was a certain Crow who thought to lead Eaglehawk along crooked routes,' began Jangamuttuk ominously.

'And later they came together as blackfellows to keep our ways straight,' retorted Waai.

'That may be so, but previously we rode our Dreaming animals, now we *are* them. It is different and difficult, for to use our hands we must transform. Why did Crow and Eaglehawk become men, but to have the use of hands?'

'Well, your transformation was incomplete and what was done had to be done. But enough of that. Last night I was Crow and went around their camp without being seen. I was just a bird, though there was that yellow-haired one who suspected me. You know, she is a *yunyi*, some sort of demon and very dangerous. I saw her kill two of them. She is also a changeling like us. She drove me away with but a glance and then behind me rose a horrible screaming and growling such as I had never heard before. That place is evil and Spirit Master entered and left without harm. We must watch him.'

'We shall,' Jangamuttuk said, 'although he is a weakling and such men are not to be feared except on dark nights when one cannot see a hurtling spear.'

'Well, he shall be rendered harmless. Now I must go and arrange a camping ground for my mob. They will be here by the afternoon and must rest and eat before the ceremony. No time must be lost. We need to hurry and construct our psychic defences, else they will grow too strong and we will never be rid of them.'

He walked off and Jangamuttuk followed him. We were left with nothing to do, for it was still morning and any preparations for the ceremony would take place in the late afternoon. Wadawaka said that now was the time to move the ship in case the ghosts returned to claim some of the goods which lay in the hold of the wreck. 'They must do it soon, or else a storm will come and perhaps detach her from the earth,' he said.

We were repairing the rigging when Jangamuttuk came to say that everything had been settled and that Spirit Master was in a more amiable mood. He also said that he had been told of a place where the schooner could be anchored in safety. Wadawaka went to see it. He returned to say that it was a sheltered cove in the shape of a deep basin with steeply sloping banks which would hinder anyone seeking to board her. 'The best thing,' he said, 'is that it lies to the west and thus away from the settlement. Now, let us shift her at once.'

The wreck still held a six-oared boat which had escaped damage by being lashed to the deck. Wadawaka got the men to untie her. She slid down the sloping deck onto the sand and we heaved her out onto the water. As the tide was on the turn and we would soon be left high and dry, Wadawaka immediately filled the boat with the fittest men and, casting off the schooner, shouted for them to tow her away towards the reef but not to attempt the passageway. Instead he had them tow the schooner parallel to the beach, towards the west. I held the helm and he never once glanced back at me, for he had told me that I was a natural steersman and could hold my own along with him. In a few hours of steady progress, we came to where the shore turned abruptly. We followed the shoreline and entered the small cove. It was as Wadawaka had described it, and the entrance was such that we would not need the tide to leave it.

'Well, it is a pretty enough place and safe too,' Wadawaka said, using the telescope to examine the steeply sloping banks of the shore. 'And deep enough,' he added. 'Look how clear the water is and how far down the bottom lies, even with the tide on the ebb.'

Leaving the schooner unguarded, as we had anchored her in the middle of the cove, we rowed back to the wreck where we scavenged some food to eat while we rested. After we had finished our meal, Wadawaka looked across at me and asked, 'Dingo, how would you like to fly with Leopard?'

'Fly?' I queried, for I was still wary of rushing through the air.

'Yes. Let us seek out that settlement and see what they might be planning.'

As he spoke his body stiffened, and watching him I felt the change come over me. The huge spotted creature snarled at me. I gave a yelp and bounded into the air, my four legs frantically working though they had no purchase. I fled up and away from the beach before I recollected myself. Still, my dingo mind was somewhat frightened when the snarling spotted shape circled me. Then a voice spoke in my head soothing me, 'Just follow me and be calm. Soon you'll be enjoying this as much as you enjoy the touch of the helm in your hands. Ease comes with use and practice.'

We flew westwards to where the schooner lay, resting peacefully in her cove. Then we lifted higher and turned east. I gave a whimper when the place where the settlement was supposed to be came in sight. I had thought that it would resemble our island mission, a house or two and a number of lesser dwellings about a central compound. Instead, there was a mass of fog or a cloud resting on the land. A smooth fantastic shape gleamed under the blue sky and the blazing sun; Wadawaka stretched out his legs and went in for a landing. His claws were extended and when he touched down, he slid for a few feet before they dug in and brought him to a halt. I followed after him, touched the white surface and skidded across it. My blunt claws failed to find purchase and I tumbled on and on until I came to rest against a buttress. I rolled away down an incline and gingerly got to my feet, the hair along my back rising and a snarl attempting to push past my tongue. There was a fetid odour of some animal, which I knew meant danger. I was about to flee when a huge white paw smashed me down upon the ice. I skidded away from a massive creature whitened all over with thick fur, with a red snarling mouth and yellow eyes. Thankfully he turned his attention onto Leopard who held a glowing crystal in his mouth. A red ray of light flashed from it to hit the creature who bellowed and charged forward. The light did not injure him in the slightest, though it enraged him. The creature would have been on Leopard in a trice, if he had not sprung into the air and retreated. With a yelp I too took to the air and rushed to his side for protection. The large white beast leapt up and fell back. He tried again and again without success. At last he gave up and, with a deep howl, ambled into the mouth of a tunnel at the bottom of the buttress I had landed against. Leopard descended to hover over the opening but a bellow from within made him retreat. We rose and studied the structure from a safe distance.

'An iceberg, though it is not possible,' Wadawaka exclaimed in my mind. 'Someone has raised a psychic shield to protect the settlement, yet it was not here last night or Crow would have mentioned it. And worse, there is that creature, a polar werebear, on guard who is immune to our crystals. Let us return and inform Jangamuttuk and Crow. We need to find other means to handle this monster.'

I followed him back to the beach where we assumed our human shapes. It was time for us to get ready for the ceremony. We did so, though Father and Crow were still absent.

'It will be difficult to get into that settlement even on the ground,' Wadawaka muttered to me. 'Let us hope that the ceremony makes us potent enough to handle bear, ice shield and those within the settlement.'

CHAPTER THIRTEEN

We didn't trust Spirit Master, nor did he trust us for we were strangers. Waai was not, but with him it was jealousy. At least that was what Waai said, explaining that for all his supposedly shamanistic powers Spirit Master's mob did not completely accept him. Of course, I did not enter the discussion. I, as usual, merely listened in to a conversation between Jangamuttuk, Wadawaka and Waai. As they talked about Spirit Master, I watched the man limp about the camp.

Waai also stared at him as he commented, 'He's neither a great hunter, fighter nor dancer and it's not only because of his gammy leg. He got that when he foolishly challenged one of the top warriors to a duel. He received a spear in the thigh for audacity and was laid up for weeks. He was a virtual outcast until he came across a whale, then a second and a third. With this, he became Whale Singer, though whether he can sing them or not is a moot point, though I must admit he can find them when they come ashore and so does have a degree of power. Still, look at him now. The great Spirit Master strutting about in his red pelt. It suits him well, but the questions are, how did he get it and how far can we trust him? Not only is he vain, but he's also a vindictive man. He is not one to forget a slight, and to get his revenge or to gain an advantage he is not above allying himself with those spirits.'

'And he is such a braggart too,' Jangamuttuk replied, wrinkling his brow as he remembered how the man had slighted him. 'Look how he acted when he was asked to participate in the ceremony about which he knows nothing. He wanted to remove songs and dancers so as to increase as he said "the psychic potency" of the overall structure. Why, he even wanted to add his own songs and dances.'

Waai smiled as he watched the man. 'Well, he is to have an important role. One which will suit him well. When I told him that he would be the climax of the ceremony, he forgot about his "psychic potency".'

'But your climaxes are not to be trusted,' Wadawaka said, with a grimace at me. 'The last time you put on this ceremony the boy suffered. He still hasn't quite recovered from it, either.'

'No harm was meant. Jangamuttuk wanted to have the ceremony and I passed it on to him. I would never do this with Spirit Master, for he lacks respect for things he does not understand.'

'Yes,' Jangamuttuk agreed, 'but will Spirit Master accept his minor role? He mentioned some sort of spirit artefact which might be shown at the conclusion, but then he remembered something which caused his mouth to gape before it closed on the subject.'

Wadawaka considered the matter, then replied, 'He is up to something. Crow, you saw him at the settlement and with a yellow-haired ghost. What was he doing there?'

'He has stumbled onto something, or his fraternising with spirits has led to his becoming their servant,' Waai hazarded, fiddling with his topknot as he thought it over. He went on, 'I saw him with that *yunyi*. They entered the settlement together, then he was ordered out by a huge spirit who smelt of carrion and blood. But then so did she and I, a crow and a lover of rotting meat, cannot fail to notice such things. Later I saw this *yunyi* kill two of those ghosts as you call them, as easily as I might throw a spear. Then she turned her bloody eyes on me and I fled away. I am certain that she sees things as we shamans do.'

Wadawaka asked, 'But where has she come from and what is she doing here?'

Jangamuttuk pointed towards the beach. 'There is the wreck of that ship and the dead crew. She must have come on that ship.'

'From where else could she have come,' agreed Waai. 'She is extremely dangerous and must be driven from this land. It is against such *moma* that the ceremony is directed, but that Spirit Master is connected to her and he is, at his insistence, the leading songman of our ceremony though he lacks a complete knowledge of it. I agreed to this because I know he lacks the power to sabotage it, as he lacks the power to bring *moma* and spirits under his control. He is, as I've said, more likely to become their servant rather than gain one as his familiar. Well, let him continue to lead the ceremony. He does a fair enough job, though his rhythm is somewhat off and as for his accent ...'

Jangamuttuk replied, 'Well, we can't slate him for that. Mine also is not of the best, though the dance steps are similar to ours and present no problem.'

'This is how he sang the opening verse,' retorted Waai, and he sang in a high-pitched voice, '*Woolla koorpana koolooloo waroo,*' then stopped and said, 'It should be lower and the audience repeats it in a higher tone. They couldn't last night. And then the second line, *meun korunna linja rooeri,* he sang it too fast.'

'Thus making us muddle our steps,' agreed Jangamuttuk.

I remembered this and how Crow and Jangamuttuk had seemed to hesitate a fraction as they came out from the shelter. I had paid particular attention to the performance and costume, for I had suddenly formed the desire of wanting also to be a master of ceremonies and appear resplendently painted with red ochre and pipeclay. Last night they had looked truly awesome. Their faces were painted stark white with pipeclay and relieved only by two red bands across the forehead and cheeks. These continued down the neck to connect up with red bands outlined in white that were painted across their chests with an oval unmarked area over the heart. They each wore armlets stuck with feathers and their hair was piled up in the shape of a soldier's helmet. Leaves had been plaited about their lower legs and these they singed over the central fire before beginning their performance. They stamped out a dance which led them to the fires marking the four quarters, at each of which a dead soldier had been re-erected in the sitting posture we had found them in. The two dancers waved the forked sticks they were carrying over the corpses, then stamped around them in an energetic dance, flicking each of the corpses with the feathered ends of the sticks. The dance ended with the sticks being thrust into the central fire.

This performance of the ceremony had much more urgency and energy than the one I had participated in on Waai's land. I was wide awake and alert when the dawn heralded the end of this section of the ceremony. It was hard to sleep and by early afternoon we were up again. It was then that I heard the elders talking.

'Now where is that fellow off to?' Waai said.

We stared at Spirit Master as, seemingly without purpose or perhaps simply to relieve himself, he wandered towards the edge of the clearing in which we were all camped. He gave a quick glance over his shoulder, then satisfied that he was unobserved hurriedly limped off into the bush.

Jangamuttuk got to his feet and exclaimed, 'Let's follow him, but not in these shapes.'

We left the camp and, when we were out of sight, changed into our Dreaming animals and took to the air to slowly circle over the bush to locate the man. We saw him making his way towards the edge of an escarpment some distance away. It was apparent that he was making straight for his goal so, to avoid detection, we flew on to the escarpment and landed on its serrated edge. We kept to our animal forms, for their senses were much keener than those of humans. Soon we caught the sound and scent of Spirit Master. We glided through the scrub and to a stand of trees from where we could obtain a view of him when he came in sight. The supposed shaman came clumping past without sensing our presence. He continued on to the mouth of a cave, hesitating as he neared it. We smelt the fear come off him and watched as he sank to his haunches and appeared to wait, though our senses told us that the cave was empty. Apart from animals and us, he was the only human about, and as for ghosts, their scent although present was stale and old. Suddenly he shuddered, but at what? All was quiet and still under the late afternoon sun, except for a lizard that scuttled from a rock and caught my attention for a second. Suddenly Spirit Master made up his mind. He got to his feet and half ran with his unsteady gait to the mouth of the cave, stopped for a fraction of a second, then darted inside. He emerged clutching an image of a female with yellow hair and pink skin. Perhaps he had indeed gained the power to petrify spirits to control them. He clasped the thing to his chest and lurched off. The others began speaking in my head.

Wadawaka declared that the object was simply the figurehead of a ship, a carved figure from wood that ghosts attached to the bows of their ships.

Waai: 'You mean that it has no magic properties but is simply a piece of wood?'

Wadawaka: 'Some seamen say that they bring good luck and help to keep a vessel on course, but that is a matter of opinion.'

Jangamuttuk: 'I felt no life within it.'

Waai: 'But he clutched it as if it were a treasured possession or might come alive in his arms. It must be more than you say.'

Jangamuttuk: 'No matter, it is what he intends to do with it that is important. Another thing, why was he so terrified to enter that cave? It seems empty, but perhaps there is something else there. Let us search it.'

Leopard, Goanna, Crow and I, Dingo, left the wood, stopped in the open and changed back to our human shapes.

'A cave is where the magician keeps the tools of his trade,' commented Waai with a laugh. He turned to Jangamuttuk and said, 'I am not interested in his trinkets, so you investigate while I go after Spirit Master to see what he does with the thing he carries.'

'If you want to, go, though what you suggest reminds me of how Crow tricked Eaglehawk into entering such a place, then closed up the entrance and rushed off after Eaglehawk's women. Well, there are parrot girls aplenty in the trees for you to seduce. So go, but remember that it is not so much that I do not trust you but that in the old stories Eaglehawk always confounds the rascally Crow.'

'But it was because Eaglehawk was greedy for the fat kangaroos my ancestor had killed that he allowed himself to be trapped. Crows are great hunters, but enough of this ... One of us should keep an eye on that fellow.'

'Well, Waai go,' broke in Wadawaka, to stop the dispute over ancient things. 'We must know what that person is planning. Now let us find out what there is in that cave. We have to hurry, for I want to go with

Jangamuttuk to spy out that settlement.' Without waiting for a reply, he fashioned a torch out of a branch and strips of bark, lit it, whirled it around to get the flame going, then stepped into the cave.

Reluctantly I followed after. I knew this cave and who had been there. Somehow I wanted to see her again, but my dingo nose had not detected her recent scent. Inside the cavern the first things we saw were some small objects wrapped in skins and bark. These would be Spirit Master's tools of trade, or of his prestige, and we did not bother to examine them. Jangamuttuk and Wadawaka might believe that the man was of no account, but he had enough knowledge to set traps such as poisoned thorns. So we left them alone and penetrated further into the cave, the reddish light of the torch flickering off the rocky walls and revealing nothing of interest until we reached the very end of the burrow. There the fluttering light of the torch showed an oblong box, the length of a man. It could not be of blackfellow manufacture; it was too smooth and well-shaped for that.

'What is this?' I ventured to ask, for as a youngster I was expected to keep my mouth shut and listen and not ask questions.

'Some ghost thing,' replied Jangamuttuk. 'It reminds me of that Fada and his boxes and trunks. Best that we be careful, for they are devious and guard their things with care.'

'That may well be,' Wadawaka agreed. 'Well, it is a simple matter to see what's inside.'

He handed me the torch and tried the lid. It slid away easily enough.

'Empty,' he said, 'but what could have been in it? Perhaps it might have contained provisions.'

'Let me see,' urged Jangamuttuk. 'Lower that torch, will you.'

He peered into the box and said, 'Only earth, but not of this land.' He took up a handful, fingered it, then sniffed it. 'Pah, it stinks of blood and rotting flesh.'

Wadawaka stared down at the box. 'I know what it is. It is a coffin, a container in which the ghosts bury their dead. But why is it here, and what has happened to the body?'

'Best we leave it,' Jangamuttuk replied. 'Who needs an empty box?'

'But why is it here?' Wadawaka persisted. 'Or how came it to be here, and what has happened to the corpse? Do you think that Spirit Master knows enough *obeah* magic to bring the dead back to a semblance of life? You and Waai say that he is a buffoon and he seems to be, but are you sure?'

'Well, let us say that he might be able to sing whales, but a spirit would entangle his feet rather than him doing the reverse, and as for corpses, he would run away if one came to life. Anyway, enough of this cave, the torch is about to go out and so am I. There's enough time left for me to see that ghost settlement.' He turned and left the cave.

We followed him and assumed our Dreaming animal shapes. I could not help but give a yelp as Leopard snarled at us to follow him. Goanna hissed and then we were in the air and flying towards the settlement. Leopard slowed as he approached the site, but Goanna sped up to take the lead. I hung back, not knowing what to expect, then ·a voice began in my head. It called to me and I wagged my tail. As soon as the settlement hove into sight, I began a long glide and landed in the compound. I looked back, expecting Goanna and Leopard to follow me but they were nowhere in sight.

I was used to such a place, as it was similar to the mission from which we had escaped. There was the compound, with the commandant's house at one corner and away from it, holding down the far edge, was another house of similar dimensions. Huts filled the lines between the two dwellings and there were a number of ghosts about, cooking over open fires. My mind was assailed by the smells and I might have slunk around searching for scraps, for the people there ignored my presence, but the command came again. I trotted towards the large dwelling, close to a fence which had been built across the width of the peninsula on which the settlement stood. In other circumstances this fence might have caused me concern, for it was higher than the height of a man and each post ended in a spike of metal, not wood. Still, it was of little interest to me for I could fly. Now the call came again and I reached the door of the house. I whined. It swung open to reveal a heavy blanket which had been placed as a curtain across the opening. I pushed my way under it and then heard the door swing shut behind me.

It was dark inside, except for the glow of a few candles which seemed to have been lit for show rather than illumination, but with my keen senses of smell and hearing I made my way straight towards a heavy chair in which someone sat. It was her! I squatted down at her feet. My head was level with her lap and I panted softly as her hand came out to stroke my head.

'Ah, little dog, you have come to see me. Good doggy, come on, you're still pup enough to settle on my lap.'

I sprang up and nestled there, pacified by the stroking hand which now shifted.

'So, you have been to my cave and with others, my naughty pet. Relax and let me peer into your mind. Ah, you like my hand stroking you there, don't you? It is pleasant and frees your mind. Now, who were those others who can assume the shapes of animals? Your father, yes, and the captain of your vessel, an African whom I have not met – as yet. I did meet your mother, another one of these shapechangers, but not so accomplished. She told me to leave you alone, but you know who your mistress is and what pleasure she can give you. I have but to call and you are eager to be with me. Perhaps I shall keep you at my side, but in this shape, not as a callow boy.'

I whined in answer to her voice which I understood in my head not through the sounds but through the projected feelings. Her stroking hand caused me to relax more and more. My eyes drooped and closed as she continued to talk in my mind.

'I like dogs and it appears that even as I now am, dogs like me. We, you and I, could hunt the night together. I shall be Kore, the virgin goddess of earth, and what fine times we shall have, especially when I succeed in getting under my control those who now roam above, unable to penetrate my psychic defences even when my powers are at their weakest. You like my hand, my servant puppy, don't you? So did my great bear, though he disliked my fangs and now he hides in his icy home protecting it from intruders.'

It was then that her stroking fingers made me shudder and she relaxed her hold. 'Now I dismiss you. Go, my pet. They are seeking you. Go, but remember you are my puppy dog.'

I felt Leopard and Goanna frantically calling out to me. I slipped off her lap, gave her hand a farewell lick and trotted towards the doorway. I went under the blanket and as it dropped to prevent the merest ray of light entering, the door swung open and I was out. Ignoring the settlement, I immediately took to the air and flew up to where Goanna and Leopard circled. I shielded my mind from them, but they were too busy communicating to each other as humans.

Wadawaka: 'The scent of the bear must have frightened him. Here he is back again.'

Jangamuttuk: 'Well, it frightened me too and our crystals have no force against it. Do you think that it could rent and tear us if we fought it?'

Wadawaka: 'I wouldn't be the one to try it, but we might have to in order to get at the settlement. Hopefully Waai's ceremony will drive it off and destroy the ice shield which protects the ghosts. Now, where is that Dingo! Keep close and don't go running off again on your own. There is evil about,' he snarled at me. I gave a yelp in feigned fright.

Jangamuttuk: 'Now we have to get back to the camp and prepare for this night's ceremony. I wonder if Crow has discovered what Spirit Master did with that artefact of his. It may be useful to us, for nothing happens without a cause.'

Wadawaka: 'All it seems to be is the figurehead of that wreck. Painted wood only.'

Jangamuttuk: 'Perhaps ... You know, at times, I miss my dreaming companion, Goanna. It was nice while flying like this to reach down and stroke his neck.'

Wadawaka: 'And I miss Leopard, even though he and I are one.'

Jangamuttuk: 'That Crow and his incomplete rituals. What does he know, except tricks?'

And so they continued to talk in their minds to each other as we made our way towards the ceremonial ground. As usual I was left out of the conversation, but now I had a secret which was my own and I could not and would not share it with them. In my mind I heard her order me to keep our relationship hidden, and I gave a whine of pleasure as I felt her psychic touch.

CHAPTER FOURTEEN

The ceremony had been structured towards an unknown climax and this resulted in a steadily building tension. Everyone felt it and such was the effect that few at the end of the fourth night could sleep. Sleeplessness in general, the presence of the bodies of the four dead ghosts who rotted and stank, though their position close to the fires did smoke them a little, and the fact that our camp was only a few yards from the wreck also added to the tension. At each and every dawn we expected a party from the settlement to appear overland or in boats to put an end to us; but they did not come and the ceremony ran its course into the fifth and final night.

This evening, after the preliminary verses, most of the men got to their feet and began to stamp out a dance step, lifting their feet high into the air and slamming them onto the soft sand. The audience sang, 'Kootoola pa renja renja; Moma, moma, pa renja renja,' the signal for the entry of Spirit Master who danced in without a trace of red ochre on him. Instead his face was covered with a slab of a mask with huge bulging eyes, a red slit of a mouth in which large sharp fangs gleamed and ears which flapped like giant bat wings. Dried grass had been attached to the sides of the mask and hung down like lank yellow hair. With his ungainly prancing, he made a perfect Moma, lurching grotesquely around the ring in a parody of a dance step as he tried to catch a victim. They easily eluded him. Then the women got to their feet and formed a square about the men, pressing them in against the devil. Suddenly the square broke and the men rushed to the shelter where they had hidden their spears. Moma was left alone in the centre of the ring. The grotesque mask bobbed up and down and twisted from side to side. The first spear whirled towards him. As the second came, he leapt from the illuminated circle and hobbled off into the darkness. More spears were hurled towards where he disappeared and might still be, but no cry of pain came.

The men rushed to the edge of the circle as the women began to sing, 'Kaea pata pata laparing kara/winna nara prinjol poronjo'. Waai and Jangamuttuk danced slowly in from the darkness whence Spirit Master had been driven. One carried the mask and the other carried the figurehead of the Kore. They circled the central fire, holding up the artefacts and shaking them over the audience. The women wailed in alarm. The men got to their feet and furiously struck their makee. Waai flung the mask into the flames and Jangamuttuk followed suit with the image. The flames leapt high, the signal for the men to pick up the four decaying ghost corpses. They held them high as they marched around the circle. The women cried, 'Ka, ka,' following them to the shelter which had been constructed to one side of the *boro* ground. The corpses were placed inside. The men now took up their shields and Waai and Jangamuttuk their forked staffs tipped with feathers. They waved these at the shelter and the men began a softer stamping .dance while calling, 'Kuh, kuh'. The two masters of ceremonies tossed their sticks into the shelter while the men continued to dance and thrust their shields towards the walls. Now both went to the central fire and each picked up two smouldering brands which they whirled into flame. They held their arms wide and danced with these back to the shelter, swung them five times about their heads then flung them inside the structure. This was the signal for the rest of the men to grab the coals of the central fire and toss them into the shelter. It burst into flames, some of which were blue. A gasp came from everyone. Then Waai danced the opening dance and the ceremony came to an end.

The stink of burning flesh quickly made most of the mob leave. Only Waai, Jangamuttuk, Wadawaka and I were left at the site which Crow informed us would in future be named, 'Spirit Burning'. It would be taboo land until the events that had happened there were forgotten, if they ever were. As he was speaking, Jangamuttuk gave a start and stared intently into the remains of the central fire where the image had been burnt. I looked too and noticed that some small objects were gleaming there.

Many of the coals had been flung into the shelter and only a few remained. Waai poked about with a partially burnt stick and carefully rolled out the shining stones.

'Silver,' exclaimed Wadawaka. 'It must have been hidden in the figurehead.'

Waai examined the silver meltings, then said softly, 'These are shaman tools. I can feel their power'.

'It is so,' Jangamuttuk agreed. 'This is a good omen for it means that our ceremony was a success. Look at that piece!'

The fire had melted the silver from whatever shape it originally might have been. Now there were a number of smaller globules and one sliver; it was this to which my father had called our attention. It was about three inches long and pointed at one end.

'Ah, silver,' Wadawaka said. 'There is a story about a shaman who was betrayed for thirty pieces of silver. Perhaps it belongs to Spirit Master?'

'No matter,' answered Waai. 'It is ours now, and I know what to do with it.'

'Are there any other stories about this metal?' queried Jangamuttuk, the Collector of Stories, of Wadawaka.

'There is one,' he replied. 'It is said that only by silver can that spirit beast which guards the settlement be dispatched, and this may be true for all I know.'

'They are our weapons,' broke in Waai excitedly. 'I will divide the smaller balls among you, but the larger one I will keep to put to good use.'

'Once,' began Jangamuttuk, 'we rode our Dreaming animals and had hands. Now we do not.'

'There is no time for that,' snapped the Crowman. 'Keep them safe as other shamans do in their bellies. Regurgitate them when they are needed. This long one I will use against the bear, but from a distance so that he will not know he is under attack until too late.'

Jangamuttuk forgot his recrimination and quickly agreed. 'This "silver" is white and of the essence of the ghosts, and that piece there which resembles a needle or a bone ...'

'I will bone the bear with it and sing him to us,' declared his fellow shaman.

'You are going to use *obeah* magic on him?' asked Wadawaka.

'It is a simple enough operation,' put in Jangamuttuk, 'and that indeed is the instrument.'

'I have the other items in my medicine bag,' added Waai. 'And now is the time to do it while the others sleep. We'll go along towards the settlement and find a spot from which we can direct our attack.'

'I'll leave you two *obeah* men to it then and go and see to my vessel,' said Wadawaka uneasily. 'Magic has its uses, but give me a solid deck beneath my feet.'

'Or the sky beneath your claws,' remarked Waai to his back.

Wadawaka went off towards the west while we went towards the east. I followed the shamans for I had never seen a boning before and my taste for such things had increased with my change. They did not object to my presence, and I knew that as long as I kept quiet and out of the way I would be allowed to observe, learning as an apprentice learns from his master, by at first seeing and listening, then by imitating.

They left the beach and went through the sand dunes to where the first of the trees began. 'This should do,' commented Crow, stopping before a banksia tree which was bent over towards the east. He cleared a small patch of ground under the inclining tree, then said, 'Now for the *munguni'*. He opened the neck of his medicine bag just enough to insert a hand, fiddled about inside and pulled out a cylinder made from the end of a human thigh bone, cut so that one end remained blocked by the socket. He unwound a piece of human hair string coiled about the cylinder of bone. One end was attached to the open mouth by some kind of black glue and to the other was attached a thin needle of bone. He detached this and replaced it with the sliver of silver, singing, *'Teri yari mungkori'* – 'The point is strong'. He went to the trunk of the tree and was about to tie the cylinder on it, when he stopped, thought for a moment, then handed it to Jangamuttuk while singing, *'Touerli yari mungkori'* – 'The container is strong'. He stretched out the string until it was taut between container and pointer and, as he did so, sang, *'Winni munnari yari mungkort'* – 'The cord is taut and strong' – finishing up with, *'Koinden kimba eno naroro'* –'Between them the life blood will flow'.

Now he squatted with the pointer held between the thumbs of his two hands, then turned and shouted to Jangamuttuk to be ready. The silver pointer began to quiver between his fingers as he chanted another song in a high-pitched voice:

> *Moma-moma kimba naroro,*
> *Munguni toka kimba naroro.*
> *Poolki, poolki!*
> *Pinjea, taro, muna munda, ho!*

'The devil's blood flows/ Into the container,/ fill up, fill up!/ Sicken, weaken, die!' The pointer leapt between his fingers as he repeated the chant. It settled towards the east and the cord tightened. The shaman chanted again. The pointer jerked in his hands, then became steady. He turned and shouted, 'Ho!' at Jangamuttuk who immediately came running to him. Waai plunged the silver needle down into the cylinder of bone and stoppered it up with some of the black gum. He wound the cord around the bone, then wrapped it up securely in a piece of possum skin.

'Got that fellow now,' the Crowman said with a grin at his Eagleman mate. 'What do we want to do with him now? He has one of those magic silver pellets deep within his heart and in that bone is the life blood from his heart.'

Jangamuttuk replied, 'We want him to stop guarding that place. He has to leave, or die.'

'Leaving, eh, now where should we send him? Into the ocean, under the ground or into the sky?'

'Down into the ocean where he can do no harm.'

'Well, we'll just do that.'

Waai lit a fire. He moved the package through the flames, saying, 'He is cold and now he has been warmed. I hear him roar as he feels something is amiss. Now he becomes warmer. Now he is hot and his body is melting away. He feels the need for the coolness of the ocean floor. Water all about him.'

He flung the package into the flames and piled wood on it. We watched as the fire blazed up and suddenly there was an explosion, a loud pop followed by a blast of steam which scattered the brands about.

'Well,' Waai exclaimed, 'he was a tough one. He held onto that place and then I felt someone trying to help him, another shaman perhaps, though he lacked my experience. My magic proved too strong and now he is gone and with him the ice shield.'

'And the settlement is open to attack and it must be done quickly, for I do not like the idea of some other shaman helping them. It is not Spirit Master, for his power is not up to it,' Jangamuttuk replied.

'Perhaps it is that *yunyi*, but no matter for she is no match for *us*,' Waai agreed. 'We have done the ceremony, broken her psychic defences and dispatched her pet. Now we can attack and on three fronts. Wadawaka can load up his boat with you lot and come in from the sea, my mob and the locals can approach from the land, and any other psychic defences will shatter under our silver when we fly in as our Dreaming animals.'

'And when will we attack? It is already afternoon and we must have time to organise,' my father queried.

'Tomorrow at first light,' his fellow shaman stated, then ordered me to collect all the remains of the fire and bury them at the foot of the tree. Before I did this, however, he poked in the ashes and recovered something which he immediately wrapped up in a piece of skin. He felt my eyes on him and after putting the package in his medicine bag said, 'A crow makes the best shaman because he has already been through the fires of creation, so watch out and see everything, but reveal nothing; hear everything but tell nothing.'

'Or else,' Father put in, 'you will see and hear nothing.'

I nodded at their wise words, though you might query whether I have kept their advice by now speaking of these events and singing the songline. But I have revealed nothing, for this past is long over. Who knows if Waai still lives? And Father has ascended into the skyworld long since. Those who remain are of the undying and we cannot be hurt by such devices. We know the signs of an attack and how to turn the magic back on the doer, but do not be afraid of me. You have your own featherfoots who protect their identity through the use of shoes made of feathers and lurk in the night to do you harm. Be wary of them, but not of me for I am not one of those that strike without advertisement, though I too belong to the dark. Settle down and listen to my tale, for my story is coming to an end as is this night. I must hurry to finish it before the dawn drives me away.

CHAPTER FIFTEEN

There are inimical forces out to destroy me. I do not know how much longer I shall be safe in this settlement which, over the last few days, has had its palisade breached on a number of occasions. My milch cows suffer a number of fatalities which the lieutenant of our ever-decreasing military detachment puts down to the depredations of the natives who seem able to enter and leave the fortified area without hindrance. I smile and agree, for he is quite under my influence. I do nothing to allay his apprehensions. I am sure that if the *Kore* had reached here safely, he would have ordered a complete evacuation of the survivors to one of the larger settlements on the far eastern coast or the southern island, but alas we have no ship and must stay here where everything is in an unsettled state. My poor native servant came to me the past night for refuge. I manage to get him to the erstwhile commandant's house, now my own, where I secret him for the time being.

He informs me, if I may use that term to cover my entering his mind, that there has been an upheaval amongst the savages and they intend to wipe us from the face of the earth. Well, I doubt that they can, though they have given him a severe drubbing. He appears quite hideous, but his very hideousness is an attraction to me. I alleviate his sufferings but do not end them, for he will prove useful if I must leave this settlement. At the moment it is the safest place for me, and perhaps I should turn some of the persons here so that I might have a more formidable force? I cannot decide and I am more concerned about my box. Some of those natives might find it and destroy it. I need to have it with me. I decide that when night falls and my strength peaks, I shall retrieve it.

I am even more determined to do this when, as I am lying in the darkness, the howls of the werebear begin and continue for some time. The poor spirit beast is obviously in pain, but in my weakened state I can do little to aid him. His cries finally cease and I know that he has been dispatched to where the spirits of all good werebears go. This upsets me, for I have been relying on him to counter psychic attacks. With his impassioned brute mind bounded by the perimeters of the settlement, which he had to defend at all costs, he was a worthy ally. Though not worthy enough, for he is gone and we now lie open to psychic attack when I am at my weakest. The strong light of day saps my strength and even though I can move about heavily draped, gloved and bonneted against the rays of the sun, it is such a trial that I do it only when absolutely necessary. So I lie here on the bed on my sprinkling of native earth and wait for the night. How good it is to feel the sun descending and my strength increasing. At last I am able to go out under the waning moon.

The men have been at the rum again and several are staggering about. The lieutenant and the Resident struggle to restore order, but they are weak and the men threaten them; that is, until I arrive on the scene. They are like brute beasts and have an ingrained fear of me. The tumult subsides and order is restored. Those who are merely inebriated slump to the ground and glower at me. I mark out one who will do for my repast later on; he is the biggest ruffian of the lot and his going should effectively break the spirit of the other troublemakers. It is of no moment to bring the lieutenant completely under my control again. He orders that a horse and cart be got ready for me. When it arrives at my door, I fling a blanket in the back and bid Renfiel to creep under it. A soldier drives me through the gate and then I send him back. It is about time that I got this servant of mine to serve.

Alone, except for the huddled figure under the blanket, I stare back at the gate where two soldiers stand on guard, keeping close together for mutual support. I lead the horse away until I am out of their sight, then I change into my bat shape and flap off into the sky. My wings go shook-shook through the air as I return to the settlement and skim over the area. There is no sign of the werebear and the apparatus, or should I say landscape, which he had constructed for his phantom shape to roam over. It is all gone. Warily I seek for traces of the attackers in the psychic realm, then use my sharpened senses to cipher out sounds, sights and even the brushings of disturbed atoms against my wings. I detect nothing and begin to feel that I am safe, though they know of the cave and my box within. My apprehension brings me back to the cart. I transform and drag the native from beneath his blanket. I thrust him behind the horse, enter his mind and give him a few lessons in keeping the beast under control. His hands are steady on the reins and he finds a joy in controlling such an animal. He thinks that he has entered a spirit realm in which he has a familiar which will guide him to what he desires most – revenge on his fellow tribesmen. Well, perhaps he shall have it, for while I have use for him he shall remain undrained.

We come to the copse of trees through which we must go to reach the entrance of the cave. There is no track and no way to force the cart through. I order my servant to stop and wait until I return. He obeys me, taking refuge under the cart with the blanket which he has grown attached to. I flit through the trees and enter the cave. All is not as I left it.

The top of my box is off. I regain my human shape for my sight can pierce the darkness. In some dread, I examine the interior of my box. I half-expect to find rude native charms left to keep me from it, but the interior remains as it was. After all there is only a layer of earth on the bottom, and how could the natives know what they are dealing with? They could only have seen a container partially filled with dirt. Now I will carry it to the cart. As I am reaching down to secure a grip, an intuition of danger flashes into my mind. At once I resume my bat shape and flit out of the cave and into a tree.

A large animal pads from shadow to shadow as it approaches the cave entrance. It comes out into the light of the moon – an African leopard, but it cannot be! Still, this is an unknown land with unknown animals, even one which can change into a man.

Under my startled gaze, this is what happens. The leopard becomes a black man, well-formed and completely naked. I gasp at his ebony beauty. He has not the rugged features or the slight figures of the local savages, but what else could he be? I examine him as he stares around warily. He looks in my direction, but his eyes are not as dark-piercing as my own and he does not see me. He changes back into the animal and slinks back into the undergrowth. I flit out and glide into the cave where I regain my form and think of him. Such a powerful physique with a deep chest, powerful torso and thick arms and legs. He will make a better servant than the poor wretch I have. I must have him; but how to take him? Should I attack as a bat or human? I decide on the human and slip off my clothing. I stand naked in the darkness, running my hands along my flanks, feeling and remembering how firm and youthful my body is. My breasts are small and rosy tipped, my long blonde hair frames a narrow face with a strong chin and eyes of startling blue, though with a reddish tinge. But what will he see, whether beast or human, except the firm whiteness of my slender figure which I was too ashamed to glory in until I came to this land? It will invite attack and he has only to bite me, to have his mouth fill with the salt taste of my blood, to become mine.

Prepared to battle and conquer, I step from the cave. My body soaks up the rays of the moon until it positively glows as a beacon calling him. He glides from the copse of trees, thankfully as a man. I open my arms and call to him. 'Sir,' I say, though he can know not English, but I hesitate to reach into his mind as yet. I am surprised and put off my purpose when he answers in return, 'Yes,' short, abrupt and wary. I must be on my guard.

'Sir,' I repeat, coming towards him, my eyes sweeping his form. Indeed, I have not been wrong about his physique. He is a perfect example of, of ... I am at a loss for words and can think only of 'savage manhood', though this, although he is naked and black, does not exactly suit him. He is not like any of these natives I have seen. He is far from Renfiel and indeed will make a worthy servant when I effect his capture.

'Sir, I am in distress,' I implore, creeping steadily nearer to him. My eyes reach out to mesmerise him for a moment before I make ready to bring my fangs into play.

Now! I spring at his neck, seeking to sink my teeth into the throbbing jugular vein while at the same instant thrusting my finger into his mouth, so that his strong teeth will clamp in agony and he will swallow my blood.

I miss my spring for instantly he changes into the leopard. I follow just as quickly with bat, but he is the faster of the two and swipes me away with a paw as I lunge at him again. His claws rip at my wing and in agony I fall to the ground, transforming into my human shape as I do so. He follows suit and, seemingly concerned, bends over me, taking care to avoid my fangs. I reach my good hand behind his head, for my other arm and hand is useless for a time. I try to tug his head down to my wounded shoulder, but he guesses my intention. However, instead of pulling back he uses my own strength against me and falls forward on top of me. I desperately struggle to release myself, but this serves only to excite him. I feel him responding to my body. Placing a sob in my voice, I implore, 'Please, sir, let me up. You are hurting me.'

'What are you, some sort of *subagu*? That's what we call such creatures as you in my language. You must have come off that ship. Why, God alone knows, but you're here and now what is to be done with you?'

His English is perfect though his skin is black, and so I appeal to the gentleman which might be within him. 'Sir, release me. I meant you no harm. I am a virgin and have been hiding here from those who would harm me.'

He makes no reply. I struggle, using all my strength in an effort to throw him off and get at his throat. It is then that he gives a grunt and I feel him enter me, tearing past whatever defences still remain and piercing me to my very vitals. I give a shriek. I have never known a man in this way and am afraid. Then I feel my body responding and try to rake his face with my nails, try to get at him with my fangs, but I am mortified when he laughs as he continues to violate me. He holds my good hand in one of his and bobs and weaves his face away from my fangs. 'No, I cannot allow you to kiss me, for it might be my last,' he says, panting slightly as he increases his rhythm.

'Sir, sir,' I pant along with him, which changes to 'master, master,' as I feel myself being overcome by an emotion I have not felt since my other dark lord took me for his then dismissed me out into my world of darkness and loneliness.

I scream long and loud and heedlessly, forgetting any pain as he throbs deep within me. This causes answering throbs which I have never known my body to be capable of. Then he groans and, from my other experience, I know that he is about to spend himself, but I have never thought that I too might reply as I am now doing. I shriek as if I am about to cease. My body relaxes under his and I feel that the sun has finally broken through to me and that I am melting away under his rays, but this is only for an eternity of a moment. The moon's rays bathe me and my wounded arm is fast recovering. I will have him yet.

'Master,' I exclaim half in earnest, 'you have conquered me and in the conquering have made me yours.'

'No,' he replies, 'I am no master nor will I have a master over me.'

His words awaken a memory long dormant. I assume a sitting position at his feet, noting how he steps back to keep himself out of my range, but I will get him to suck my blood yet. I do not want to use him for sustenance, for he must pay for what he has done to me, though in the doing he has awakened a yearning for a companion to share my life and the hunt. Since my dark lord went I have been too long alone. And now I remember who he is.

'Sir,' I exclaim, 'your quotation gives away your secret. know who you are, for that was the very thing you said when you were the talk of London when Granville Sharp, the abolitionist of all that makes men slaves, made you free and by so doing freed all such as you. I know the case which went before the King's Bench well, for my father laboured in the Serjeant's Law Inn for Bull Davies who fought his case with his eloquence. He wrote the disposition which set you free and Lord Mansfield declared you a black Englishman unable to be enslaved. Summer, later baptised with the Christian name of John, is who you are, but how come you appear so young, for that was – time has little meaning for me – some decades ago I think.'

'What is that name to me? I was a slave with a slave's name and believed that I walked free. We Africans in England did indeed achieve a liberty, as poor blacks to be rounded up and sent to Sierra Leone in Africa where we were to govern ourselves. At the first, I was part of that ill-fated expedition, from which mercifully I was relieved. The goodly philanthropists in charge hoarded the money which was to be used to provision us for the ordeal ahead. I remonstrated, was dismissed from my post, called to account for embezzlement and instead of returning to my

African home, I found myself transported as a convict to this far land. Such is freedom when it is given by others.'

'And so you have reverted to the savage, sir! Once you were given the appellation of gentleman. It seems that you have gone from slave to gentleman to convict and back to savage. Perhaps it is time to recover the gentleman since you have dishonoured me and must make amends, else you are only worthy of being a slave or in your natural state a savage.'

'I am no English gentleman. I have seen what they do and spurn the station I once desired. And how is it that you claim to be the ravished woman when you are a human no longer? You are a *subhaga*, one who rises to suck blood. You shed your skin so that you never grow old and fly through the sky as a bat. You are no longer human and for all I know you have stolen that body you wear.'

'And what of you, master, and your secrets? Why do you not grow old as other men? When we were joined, my mind entered yours and I saw a woman lurking within. Who is she, for I have seen the beast which snarls, though not the snake. What are you, for you are more than human, that is why I call you master.'

'Question me and I will not answer. When the heart sees, the mouth does not speak, nor does the *subhaga* acknowledge a master. It is beyond her nature as it is mine.'

'But it was in your nature to savage me. Well, you took what you desired, but in the taking took me. So be it: I will be your companion. Side by side we can rule this vast land. I with the fire of your sun in my veins; you with the coolness of my moon in your veins. We supplement each other, the dark and the light, and we can make this land ours.'

'Enough of this, I am ...'

'A mouth sprouting empty words. He who refuses to be a master is now the master of a vessel, just as he who refused to be a slave became a convict. Well, what of this vessel you see before you?'

'I help only those who needed help, and when I have done I will be master no longer.'

'And do I not need your help? The settlement is in dire straits. If it is destroyed I may well be too. You must aid me, for my father laboured to free you. It was his work that set you free and see how you have repaid him ...'

'Enough of that settlement which rests on stolen land. If it survives so be it, but I think that it is past saving, as is the institution of slavery. They murdered the innocent inhabitants and must be brought to justice. It shall be done, but it is of little concern to me. I have been forced to become a wanderer, for where is there a place that I might rest and call my own? I was born on the ocean and drift with the tide. Once I was called Summer, but I am Wadawaka, "Ocean Born".'

He is stubborn, but my conversation distracts him with memories and feelings which disarm him. He stares into the night, reliving ancient memories and hurts. My hand flashes up and my nails rake his skin. I bite my lower lip with my own fangs and spit blood at him. He twists aside his face and then I am on him. I struggle to make him mine, but he has the strength of a leopard and also its lust, for before I know it he is in me again. I am raised to heights and lowered to depths that I have never known, even in my wildest kill, that of Torrens the werebear. As I approach my climax, I am in my bat form hurtling at the sun, not caring if I dissolve in the blast of light. Then I shudder and find myself in his strong arms. It is over and too soon for both of us. How reluctantly he pushes me away. It is as if he would pull me closer and enjoin with me a third time. I too wish for his love and will have it again, for I know that I have gained him somewhat.

'Thank you, master,' I murmur, gently mocking him as I lick my bloody lips. 'I taste my own blood here, but when I reach down with my fingers then raise them to my mouth, I taste also your white blood.'

As I say this, I glance at his chest and see that in my passion I have ripped his skin. I touch the scratch with my fingertips, then suck them. 'Now I have too the taste of your red blood. It is a pity that you do not sample mine, for then we would be truly united as once I was with that dark lord who made me as I am.'

'Enough of lords and masters,' the African exclaims. 'Enough, for we do not need anyone over us. We are free beings.'

'Yes, but perhaps there is a fate which has brought us together, and does it not affect that freedom you cherish? Even now, I peer in to your mind and find there that same strange weakness and need which drew me to my lord, though I wished otherwise. You cannot escape me, for I am what you desire.'

'Are you?' he queries in a gruff voice, then changes into his magnificent animal form and confronts me with a snarl as if in anger. Even though I know he will not harm me, I still draw back. Our eyes meet and I find the answer to his question there, before he springs into the air and speeds off.

As my eyes follow him I become aware of the lightening sky. Our encounter has used up the night and I am trapped here until the evening. Still, my exertions have introduced a delightful lassitude which urges me to my box. How peaceful the cave is and how dark. I move the lid of my coffin and recline within. The loam of my earth lulls me and my mind drifts to the African then past him to my father. He who brought me into the world and worked to free John Summer so that his daughter could meet him. Yes, fate enmeshed these actions to that of my dark lord who, taking my life blood, bequeathed to me a life beyond life which led me to this land and to him.

I feel again that urge which drew me then, a callow girl, out of the safety of her dwelling and into that desolate piece of land where he was waiting. I remember how he said to me that such a life as he had was long and to endure it something more was needed than mere blood-taking. 'A purpose?' I had queried as I half swooned in his arms. 'Or a person,' he had replied. 'It does not matter, for there is an eternity to fill.'

It was then that I glimpsed his mind and the ancient trials that he had performed and the cruelties he had practised. I might have felt tainted by such deeds except that the dark joy that at times pervaded the doing of them was similar to what I experienced as he drained my body while I begged him not to leave me, kneeling in submission at his feet as I hesitated to draw a little of his blood in return. How young I was, knowing only my mother's urging to be as she was, a respectable wife. Well, perhaps this past night I have had a taste of wedded bliss with one who has a longing in him which calls me to him as I call him to me – or do I but imagine it? Well, my life is long and I will follow that John Summer for love or vengeance, one or the other, for they are much the same.

I seek to reach out to his mind but recoil in dismay. They are planning to attack the settlement and here I lie, trapped in my box, unable to face the strength of the day. There is no way for me to hinder them and I fall into thoughts of revenge. He tricked me away from the settlement and for that he will not escape me.

CHAPTER SIXTEEN

Waai squatted after outlining the plan of attack in the sand and invited an elder to speak about the occupied peninsula. The elder got to his feet, a bunch of killing spears clutched in his right hand and his narrow shield in the left. He began: 'You know in the old days when the land had arisen from the sea and became inhabited, the birds and animals living on it became annoyed that the sea animals still came ashore as if they owned the place. This made them wild and so they held a great meeting, just as we are holding a meeting now, and even then they were called together by Crow who went from mob to mob. Goanna was there, so was Copper Snake which is my totem, and so was Turtle, that fellow there. We decided then to attack the sea creatures when they came ashore. We kept to the plan. At the forefront was Turtle, who might be slow but carried a strong shield. The fighting was fierce and in the battle he was badly wounded, for he had followed them out to sea where he was also at home, though he loved the land more because he was born in it. Well, with his life ebbing away, he came ashore where that peninsula is and stretched out. That long piece of land is his head and neck, beyond it is his body. This is why we call the place *Poopikapi,* Turtle Head, and now, as in those days, it is time for us to drive these sea creatures away.'

His speech was followed by the clash of spear against shield. The mob who were to attack from the land moved out along the beach towards where the sun was writhing above the horizon.

The previous afternoon Wadawaka had taken the long boat and some men and rowed to the schooner. We raised the anchor and, with the long boat fastened behind, Wadawaka took the helm and sailed her out from the basin and eastward along the shoreline. We reached the beach where the wreck lay and anchored offshore. From there we would sail her the next morning to the peninsula and use the long boat to land. That night Jangamuttuk sang his songs for success, while Wadawaka went to reconnoitre the settlement. He returned with the sun and it seemed that his mind was elsewhere. Still, he checked the schooner and all was ready by the time the mob moved off along the beach. Our mob was already aboard. Wadawaka upped anchor and tacked along the shoreline. The sea was calm and the slap-slap of waves against our hull made us calm also. I checked the priming of my pistol, just in case I was in the landing party, while the others sharpened their spears. Ludjee, who was the only woman aboard for we had left the others at the camp, watched the proceedings, then sat down and went into a trance.

Jangamuttuk began singing a verse from the *Moma* ceremony which would dissipate any baleful psychic forces. He sang, '*Oraki manilla molla manilli. Oraki manilla molla manilli,*' then stopped and said, 'And this is how you send those ghosts on their way,' and sang, '*Kootoola parenja renja/kuntien polooloo wollum poomara/kara pata pata lapa ringkara/winna narra prinjol poronjo.* Arrh, I have sent them on their way. Now all we have to do is to clean up the place.'

It was then that Ludjee came out of her trance to report that she had been over the settlement. 'Poor things,' she said, 'they are upset about a missing person and are off guard. They do not want to be there and so it is right for us to send them back to where they belong.'

Wadawaka swung the schooner in towards the side of the peninsula. It seemed that they did not expect anyone to come from the sea and there was no challenge as the anchor dropped and those who were going ashore got into the long boat. Wadawaka stared at the settlement site, but he would not land. He stayed aboard with Ludjee, Jangamuttuk and myself. As the boat neared the shore there were shouts from the settlement and then screams. Wadawaka gave a start and said to himself, 'A bad business, but it can't be helped.' He turned away and stared over the sea.

We were excited about what was happening on shore and assumed our animal shapes to fly over the place in case we were needed. Jangamuttuk held one of the silver balls in his mouth and Ludjee one in her hands, but there was no use for them. The collection of huts and the two houses were bare of all psychic interference and the battle was merely physical. I watched as a long spear found the chest of a soldier and then saw the warrior rush in and deliver him a tremendous blow with his *nulla-nulla* club, caving in his skull.

I landed and trotted towards the house where the lady had been. I did not want her to be killed along with the others. I hesitated to watch as a ghost woman was thrown down and had her throat hacked with a stone knife until her head parted from her body. The warrior rose with a shout and held the head aloft. Blood dripped over him. This made me fear for my mistress's safety and I loped into the house, undaunted by the humans who were more intent on slaughtering each other than in noticing an animal. I slunk into the darkened interior. It was empty. I sniffed around, casting for her scent, but she had not been there for some hours. She was safe, and glad at heart I made my way outside where the fighting had ceased.

There had been about forty ghosts inside the fence, among them six women. All were dead. I went from body to body, seeing how the long spears had passed through them and how most of the heads had been bashed in by heavy clubs. Such was the surprise, or the despondency, of the settlers that I had not heard a single musket fired. I trotted towards the gate following an old scent of my lady. The gate gaped open. Beside it two red-coated soldiers lay with the backs of their heads bashed in. They still clutched their muskets, but had not even had the time to prime their weapons let alone fire them. Now that I had seen all that I wanted as a dingo, I resumed my human shape and walked back towards where the mob of blacks were gathered about Waai. They were all excited and the warrior still clutched the woman's head by her long black hair.

Waai shouted, 'It is all over and they are gone from these shores. Now we must burn their bodies and their dwellings. Get rid of all traces of them ever being here.'

The man with the woman's head swung it around and around and let go. It described an arc, hair streaming behind and fell within the doorway of the house of my lady. Now the men rushed about in a frenzy, collecting bodies and flinging them into the two houses and the huts. Anything lying in the open which belonged to the ghosts followed them. At last there was nothing left of the settlement except the dwellings and the bloodsoaked ground. I felt sad and even choked back tears as I saw the first of the pathetic huts catch. Men ran with brands snatched from the ghosts' cooking fires and flung them into every structure. Flames rose high into the air and with them came the smell of roasting flesh, human flesh. Perhaps as Dingo I might have enjoyed the reek of burning bodies, but in my human form this repelled me. I even vomited as from one of the houses came groans as a ghost, assumed dead, regained consciousness to find himself being burnt alive. Worse, from one of the larger dwellings rushed one of them with his clothes afire. He ran aimlessly about until the men, as if after a kangaroo, chased him and ran him back towards his funeral pyre. He collapsed before he reached it. Long spears were used to push the smouldering corpse back into the burning house.

The scene was too much for our mob and they returned to the long boat and pushed off to the schooner. We were followed by the stench of burning meat, and when we clambered up we found the three there gazing at the shore.

'It is time that we were off while the wind is favourable,' Wadawaka said quietly. Then he turned to ask me, 'Was she there?'

'No,' I replied, knowing who he meant.

'That's perhaps not for the better for she is the worst of the lot, but what is done is done.' He turned away and ordered the anchor up and the sails unfurled. We moved away under the impetus of a land breeze and soon were well out to sea. Behind us long columns of smoke rose into the sky and, whipped by the breeze, turned and chased us with the smell of those burning bodies. At last it disappeared and we scudded along under a favourable wind.

We aimed straight towards the mid-afternoon sun, where it writhed in the sky. A crow came from the distant shoreline to perch upon the main mast of our vessel. He gave a few caws of farewell, then rose, circled the deck, shat and almost hit Jangamuttuk, then flapped off back towards the land. Wadawaka was at the helm and seemed to be thinking deep thoughts, so I left him alone. After the massacre everyone was too quiet and pensive for my liking, though they should have been happy to be continuing the voyage. At last, bored, I became Dingo and rose into the air, feeling as free as I ever could be. On the horizon was the smudge of smoke of the burning settlement. I sighted on it, but to the left. Now I was over the coastline and heading towards the serrated edge of the plateau. I located the cave and hovered over it. She was not there, but then I saw leading away from the copse of trees the twin runnels of the wheels of a cart. I followed them along and reached the horse and cart, slowly making its way westwards. I stretched out my legs and in a moment was on the ground. I smiled as I remembered my previous clumsiness, then I loped after the cart, taking the arc of a circle which brought me out in front of the horse. I squatted there and stared at Spirit Master at the reins. I raised my muzzle and gave a howl which startled him. I was pleased to receive the scent of his fear. I knew that I could spring at his throat if I wanted to, but there had been enough killing and he was with my mistress. I sat there and watched him jerk on the reins to make the horse break into a trot. The cart rattled past and I saw that it carried an oblong box. I fell in behind and loped up to the tailgate. From the box came the perfume of stale blood and rancid flesh. I snarled in joy for within lay my mistress, safe and sleeping away the lassitude of the day. She did not stir and would not emerge to pat and caress me. Disappointed, I gave a long howl, then took to the air and flew off to the coast. There on the sea moved our schooner under full sail, aiming straight into the coils of the falling sun.

I landed on deck and became George. Wadawaka was still at the helm and I went to him. We exchanged glances and he gave me the wheel without a word. The course as always was westward, ever westward. I held her steady on the sun, not even glancing away from the bows as Wadawaka became Leopard and flew off towards the land. I hoped that he might have better luck than I had. In my mind I felt her come awake and I began singing the first verses of the *Song Cycle of the Nomad*:

Wadawaka inenanam modjie modjie,
Djurin nana gulara bidin
Dabor inganj bidin
Djao djao.

'He came from the sea, from the cool, cool sea, he rose to hurry us west.'
But this begins another yarn and I have not the time to begin, let alone continue it, for the dawn is close at hand and it is time for me to go. I thank you for listening to my story and helping to alleviate my solitude, for it is difficult for one like me who lacks a home and must wander through the night seeking friendly campfires such as your own. Now I must go, for I feel the first burnings of the light upon my skin. It has been some time, a long time, since I have seen the sun writhing in the sky, but the moonlight is soft on my skin and she is enough for me. I go and perhaps one evening I will return to sing and relate to you the *Song of the Nomad*. I will exact something in return, but do not be afraid – I am not that greedy!

www.ingramcontent.com/pod-product-compliance
Lightning Source LLC
Chambersburg PA
CBHW031207260626
47169CB00004B/1286